C000049539

Bee Write

2023

Copyright ©2023 The Hive

All rights reserved.

"Bee Write 2023," published through Young Author Academy.

Young Author Academy FZCO

Dubai, United Arab Emirates

www.youngauthoracademy.com

ISBN: 9798861074162

Printed by Amazon Direct Publishing.

No part of this publication may be reproduced in whole or in part, or stored in a retrieval system, or transmitted in any form, by any means, electrical, mechanical, photocopying, recording or otherwise without the prior written permission of the author.

Contents

Why Fit in, When You Were Born to Stand Out

by Anika Sharma

Once upon a time there was a boy named Jack. Jack was very different from others, he didn't make good friends. While other kids would play cricket he would scribble on his note book and do amazing drawings. All the other kids were making fun of him and calling him a nerd, loser and a boring boy. Jack didn't like this but he would ignore them and just draw his favorite animated characters like Sniper wolf, Pikachu and the Last Dragon.

One of his finest paintings he made was of him and his mother when he was a baby. He drew himself and his mother when she cuddled him in his crib. He gifted the same to his mother on her birthday. She had loved it and she put it in the living room and everyone who visited their home admired the painting.

A few years passed by and Jack grew up into a fine artist. Some of his paintings marveled at the art galleries. He became the most popular artist, like Pablo Picasso. All friends who made fun of him went to see his art gallery and admired it.

Some of the friends felt bad the way they treated Jack and apologized to him for their rude behavior. They would often visit his art exhibitions and purchase his paintings. Jack had proved that his passion for art was not wrong and he followed his passion. He even started his own art school where he would guide young kids to follow their passion and do whatever their heart desires.

Jack followed his dreams of being an artist and in all this, he realized how people change and he smiled within and thought of the famous quote

by Dr. Seuss –

"Why fit in when you were born to stand out."

Put-Outer

by Jilliane Alinan Baldonado

During dusk's appearance,
occurs a pitiful lament.
Poisoning my brain;
I give in for a moment.

A fickle mind's despair,
bitterness on the tongue.
Mind beyond repair,
its ambitious deed; done.

It is life's essence
to be happy or unhappy.
Perpetual emotions;
a never-ending story.

I sat simply in defeat,

cold and alone.

Words I utter and repeat,

a flicker of hope returns.

With a little click,

it took and gave back: light.

My Deluminator

shines bright on the darkest night.

—J.A.B

Inspired by the quote,

"Happiness can be found, even in the darkest of times, if one only remembers to turn on the light."

–Harry Potter and the Prisoner of Azkaban by J. K. Rowling

Fireflies

by Maria Theres Kizhakkuden

A deep pit;

all darkness with no sound.

i am hidden.

no one hears me, i hear no one,

no one but my own self

telling me truths

(or maybe just lies?)

the pit seems darker,

the pit seems deeper,

with every thought i hear:

'you were once alive,

now you're dead.'

there's no hope for me,

for a chance of living as I once lived.

"the dead can be risen darling," she whispers.

the dead can be risen, so can i.

'but the pit is inescapable,
stay in the dark.
she isn't even here –
your mind is tricking you.
she doesn't know you.'

she's willing to try, so am i.

the walls start to crack.
a little opening for me,

a little light.

one orb squeezes through,
and another and another.

they flutter around me. it's okay. it's safe.

Emotionless

by Bethany Fernandes

"NUMBING THE PAIN FOR A WHILE WILL ONLY MAKE IT FEEL WORSE WHEN YOU FINALLY FEEL IT,"

J. K. ROWLING, HARRY POTTER AND THE GOBLET OF FIRE

A robot. That's what they call me. Emotionless. That's what they emphasize. I'm a thinker, not a speaker. Afraid of the "warmth" I'm bound to receive after opening up. Is it the warmth of love? Or is it the warmth of the devil welcoming me into the realm of pain? It's always "Why don't you ever open up?" or 'Stop bottling those emotions" but mainly 'You're so strong for that".

Truth be told, I don't think I'm strong. Quite the opposite. I think I'm a coward, a weakling. Ironic, isn't it? The way those girls cry on my shoulders, the way they tail me with their problems, and the way they look up to me. Look up to me? I look up to them. How can one be ready to tell all of their problems and feel all that pain? More importantly, how does one heal from that pain after finding comfort in another?

I don't want to feel pain, I don't want to break that bottle of emotions into pieces and I don't want to feel ready to accept the truth. So I'll hold it in, I'll numb it, and I'll endure each sharp stab of the problem I face, piercing into my soul. That agonizing cramp of problems and emotions surging through my body from bottom to top... I'll endure it all. Even though it truly hurts, even though it feels like my soul is being torn apart. The pain I feel now will never amount to the pain felt from letting it out. But numbness doesn't last. One day, I'll burst.

My bottle will shatter, the truth will be revealed. And I won't feel pain from the problems, I'll feel a pain much worse. The pain when people find out who I truly am, what I truly hold behind the flesh and bones. The pain when people turn away. Those who I once held so close to my heart, Afraid of my emotions. The emotions expressed by someone who had appeared so emotionless. This type of pain cannot be bottled up like the others.

Broken Soul

by Rachel Joanna Ediriweera

You want to feel free. You want to change. But your heart, your aching heart, holds onto the past. It clings to it so tightly it hurts. You hold onto the past, scared leaving it will change you. And not in a good way. You numb yourself with all sorts of distractions. Social media, food, isolation. You do this for so long you can't feel anymore. You can't think anymore. You don't know how it feels to be free. You're locked up in a prison in your mind, waiting for someone to let you out. But...who?

It's mad to think how long I've gone through the same cycle. Wake up, eat, cry, repeat. I don't know why I feel like this. I can't find the source. It's just not in my code. Not in the way the universe planned my life. High school feels like a chore. Waking up feels like a chore. Living feels like a chore. I've tried all the options: journaling, yoga, therapy, and meditation. Nothing could mend the pieces. I know what I sound like. Every depressed teen in every high school movie. She finds a boy and feels happy. There. Happily, ever after. That's not how reality works, unfortunately. Not in my universe. Not in my world.

To add context, no I am not depressed. I wasn't diagnosed with it anyway. Just that sad, dreadful feeling that pulls you down the sea. And there's no way to remove it. No way to remove the chains. But only with a key. I honestly laugh at people who are so optimistic. So energetic and says life is amazing and that stuff. It isn't. No one I knew died, and no one called me out. I've just been like this. I'm just built like this. You don't need a reason to be sad. You just are.

So, I'm sixteen and surviving high school. Pretty basic really. Nothing fun, exciting or worth talking about happens. Nothing new at all. That's what drives me insane. Repetition for years. I feel like I'm living in a simulation. Just an NPC following codes blindly. So, what ticks my tock? I'm still figuring that out. Still writing my life novel. Still walking the path that leads me to my destiny. But what destiny do you have when you don't know yourself?

My mum and dad are champs. Absolutely successful. They try so hard to let me speak my feelings out. They want to help me. They try to turn the lock. To unlock my prison. But I prevent that. I lock them out, yet I love them more than words can describe them. It's a confusing feeling. Love yet pushing them. It gives such a weird, horrid feeling in my gut that it makes me sick. My head spins. My heart beats faster than I can blink. Yet I still do it.

I'm no bad egg, just to point it out. I don't know what am I. Do you know those stereotypical groups at school? The jocks, athletes, nerds, artists, drama kids, popular, and gothic. I just don't fit in any one of them. I don't fit into school at all. I have one friend, and it's just by choice. I don't like a group of people. More than two is a swarm. Too many relationships. Too many possibilities of heart breaks. Her name was Sage. She was imperfect like me. Sad. But, with a bit more hope, shining in her eyes than me. Little bit more joy. A little bit more open. I remember what she told me before, 'imperfection is perfection. It's practically in the name'. I felt so free. So open-minded with her. I could share anything that my heart desired and feel no pain.

It was pleasant to have her. Like a wave she was. Calm yet powerful. Yet, after the day was gone, I was back in my messy room, covered in layers of blankets and listening to music. Music is therapy. It's like a gift every time you play it.

Play the right ones, you're lost in a new world. A world in your imagination. Where you are the one in play. You know, I'm not all that boring actually. I have a habit of writing a poem or two. I would pick a pen and write to my heart's content until I have nothing left inside of me to write about.

Numb little bug
Oh, you're so sad
You hide in your corner
Yet you're not that bad
Numb little bug
You distract yourself with things
You want to forget your past
Oh, will you help me, please?

It's my way of relaxing. My way of feeling like I'm floating. Floating on grey clouds, covered in a layer of rain as I see the world below. It's so tiny compared to being inside.

You know, I heard a quote from somewhere. Or maybe from my head. 'Numbing the pain for a while will only make it feel worse when you finally feel it'. It made me think. For the first time in years, I'm thinking. I like to numb myself. It makes me feel safe, so I won't feel pain. But now that I realized it, it might be the opposite. Pushing mum and dad. Suffocating in my tiny bedroom. Choking myself underwater. Isolated. I want to resurface back. I want to be able to breathe again. Maybe I don't need a key. Maybe I have it in my palm ready to unlock my chains. But I'm not using it. I'm letting myself drown. Letting myself sink underwater until there is no light left to be seen. No fight left in me. If only I can just reach for the lock. May I will be able to breathe again.

What if we're right? Maybe it's ok to be sad. It's ok to cry... go cry. Go and shout your feelings. I'll be next to you, ok? You're fine. You're ok. I'll be right by your side.

RIO, OH RIO!

By Drei Patrick Apigo Rosete

Rio was born like any other pigeon. He hatched out of an egg, looked around. He was in a tree, full of other pigeons flapping and cooing about. He didn't think much of himself. He thought that he was just an ordinary pigeon, and he was useless, like all the others. "Coo Coo! Coo! Hello, fellow birds! Coo Coo!" Rio's mother arrived with some fat, juicy worms. "You better eat these, so you can grow up to be a big and strong pigeon, just like your brothers!"

Several years passed by. By this time, Rio was already in bird school. That was when he discovered his talent. He was brilliant at flying. He could do a lot of tricks, and he flew fast! Rio was very excited for the day when they get to pick their clubs. The options were Drama Club and Flying Club! If Rio joined the flying club, he could improve his skills and get better.

The day came when they could pick their clubs. "All right now class," said Mr. Eagle. "Whose going for Flying Club?"

Only Rio's wing went up. "Ok... Whose opting for Drama Club?" All the other wings went up. "Pffft.... Rio, Oh Rio! Why is Rio going for Flying Club? That club is for wimpy birds only."

Stacey, the class bully, laughed at him. It might be a surprise, but Stacey was a boy eagle, although Stacey is a girl name. Rio was offended. He thought, since everyone is going for Drama Club, I guess I'll go for that, too! Rio raised his wing. "Excuse me Sir, but I'd like to change to Drama Club!"

Mr. Eagle looked surprised. "Why, Rio? You're very good at flying! Remember, just because everyone is opting for Drama Club doesn't mean you opt for it too! Rio, you don't need to fit in.

You must value your talents, not think about the other talents! But if that's your wish, I'll change your name to Drama Club, alright?"

Rio didn't make a second thought, although he felt sad and uncomfortable about choosing drama club. He wanted to fit in with the class, and he didn't want to look like a wimp in front of Stacey.

Drama Club was so boring. Rio was starting to regret his decision. Mr. Tate, the Drama teacher, would always scold Rio for falling asleep when he was teaching. "Rio, Oh Rio! Really Rio, you could've just picked the Flying Club! You are a disgrace to the Drama Committee!"

Rio was kicked out of the Drama Club, and he went to Flying Club instead. There, he never fell asleep. He was taught new tricks, and, in a few days, he nailed the obstacle course! Rio was proud of himself, and he didn't care what the others thought. Every day when Stacey would come by and make fun of him, Rio would just shout, "AT LEAST FLYING IS USEFUL!"

Stacey stopped making fun of Rio, and they day came for the final exams. Rio's flying exam went first, and the whole class had to come and watch. Rio had to fly through an insane obstacle course with rings of fire, falling items, and extreme weather! Astonishingly, he got through the course in 10.57 seconds! The whole class except Stacey cheered, "Hooray for Rio!"

Next was the Drama exam started, and the whole class had to do a play named A Midsummer Night's Dream, by William Shakespeare. Rio got to sit down and watch. It was a complete disaster! Everyone forgot their lines, they mixed up their costumes, and the backdrop was wrong! As Rio's classmates were flapping around the stage helplessly, Rio smiled. He chuckled and said to himself, "Now I get it. Why should I fit in with the class, even though I don't feel happy but because everyone's going with it? I guess I should have listened to my talents. I guess I was born to stand out all along!"

Changing Colour by Emotions of a Dog

by Yawna Barkil

Chapter - 1 'Who is Daisy?'

One morning, a girl called Nazly was playing with her dog. This dog was called Daisy. Nazly got Daisy at her seventh birthday. Daisy, the very cute doggy wasn't ordinary like all the other dogs, she was ... special!

Daisy could change colour when her feelings changed! (That is why Nazly calls her the CC Dog: changing colour dog), for an example if she is frustrated or mad, she will turn totally RED. The amazing PEACH colour would come when she is feeling hungry.

Isn't that a spectacular thing for such a dog to have as a gift?!

Only one thing left to know about this little furry dog. Daisy didn't tell any of the other dogs about it. yep! She kept it as a secret. Only Nazly knew about it. Do you know why she didn't tell anyone?

That's because she thought that if she tells her friends all those feelings that she was passing through... her fear, excitement, her anger... they would laugh at her; they won't understand and accept her as she was.

She felt happy about being special but, still a bit sad about shining more than the other stars in this wonderful huge sky. Despite Nazly telling her that she should trust and accept her gift the way it is, she still felt blue. She believed that she had a roll in the world, but she was scared as she didn't understand it yet.

Chapter - 2 'Daisy's Mission'

One day, Nazly heard a strange noise coming from a dark green bush. There was a piece of metal with two buttons on it. Near it was a note that said, "Dear little girl, do you wish to explore emotions? then press the green button."

Did you know that the metal thing and the note was from Nazly's mum?

Yes! Mum wanted everyone to know about Daisy's special gift and she wanted Daisy to know it was ok to shine more than the other stars.

After Nazly read the note, she pressed the green button. Suddenly, seven rainbow-coloured doors appeared before her. She read the instructions. All she had to do now was to guess the emotions behind the doors, and..... EXPLORE!

All of these colours were there: RED, ORANGE, YELLOW, GREEN, BLUE, PURPLE and finally... PINK!

Nazly couldn't figure out any of them. A lightbulb suddenly lit up in Nazly's head! Daisy could help her guess the seven emotions! She went to find Daisy sleeping on her bed. "I need you to help me figure out the feelings." Nazly told her all the instructions that needed to be followed.

"Alright" Daisy replied as they went outside.

"What is Red?" asked Nazly, pointing at the RED door. Daisy thought and said "angry!" and they kept on going till they finished.

ORANGE-nervous, YELLOW-surprised, GREEN-sick, BLUE-sad, PURPLE-excited, PINK-shy.

Nazly and Daisy looked at each and every room meanwhile....... Some kids and their dogs were WATCHING everything. "OH NO!!!" cried Daisy, "Now, everyone knows my secret!

Chapter-3 'Bye-bye Daisy'

"Oops!" said Nazly, pushing the other kids away.

"Why are you pushing us?" asked Roger surprised (ROGER is Nazly's friend).

"Daisy was amazing! We love her gift," said Lolo, Roger's dog.

For the first time Daisy was feeling proud and happy ... she wasn't scared and shy anymore that she finally accepted and understood what was her role and what she will stand for.

Daisy apologised, that she is now able to deal with her emotions.

My story is inspired by the quote below,

"PROMISE ME YOU'LL REMEMBER, YOU ARE BRAVER THAN YOU BELIEVE, STRONGER THAN YOU SEEM, SMARTER THAN YOU THINK."

-WINNIE THE POOH by A. A. MILNE

Medusa

by Qazi Ali Ahmed

I rushed down the forest, my heart in my mouth and my brain whizzing. 'Who were these people?' I thought.

"Were they here to steal back Medusa?" I investigated my pocket for the important launch codes, glad to find them still there. Admiral Ross was right; Dmitri was sure to send men to steal the codes, I was an idiot for not stashing it.

I jumped behind a tree to catch my breath. A hoarse voice rang out behind me, "Give me the codes Jake, we don't have to do this the hard way."

I turned around to see the speaker and was met with four eyes staring right back at me. It was Dimitri and his side-kick Maxim. "You may have outmanoeuvred my men at your house and killed them, but I know better."

It was true, I rigged the house to explode using the oven when I realised I was being attacked and escaped to the woods through a window. I ran down to the creek, desperate to escape Dimitri's cold grasp. A shot rang out behind me and chopped my ear lobe. I exclaimed at the sudden pain and grasped my ear, drenching my palm with blood. I ducked behind a log fearing another bullet would come. It was clear Dimitri wasn't going to let me go at all, I had to defeat him at his own game. I had to take him on.

I heard footsteps behind me and peeked through a hole. Maxim was slowly pacing his way through the dry leaves towards me holding a revolver anxiously. To kill Dimitri, I was going to need to make the playing field even and that was possible only through killing Maxim. I knew just what to do. I came up from my hiding spot with my hands on my head, surrendering myself to Maxim.

"You made the right choice Jake," said Dimitri lowering his revolver and trying not to hide a squeal of joy. Maxim reached his hands into my pockets with the intention of finding the codes and when I was sure he was covering up Dimitri's view I made my move. I struck Maxim on the forehead with my palm and snatched the revolver from his grasp; Dimitri, suddenly alarmed, aimed his revolver at me but I flew behind the log and shot Maxim dead in the face, splattering blood everywhere. Now it was only me and Dimitri, but I was still not out of the fire yet.

Dimitri was angry with the death of his favourite assistant and took his rage on me. In anger he shot at the log, filling it with holes but luckily none through me but I decided to play along. I filled the air with my groans and gave the impression that I was shot. Dimitri, surprised, rushed over to the log to see what he had done, too over-confident to understand the plot.

He peered over the log and was met with a bullet straight through his neck. He gagged and grasped his neck and tried to comprehend what had happened, he swayed with the air until his legs finally gave in and he crumpled to the floor. He too, had been outplayed like his men by me and I finally guaranteed security for Medusa once and for all.

A Little Tale of a Little Girl

by Kaira Teresa D Silva

Seussville, a town unlike any other, named after the famous author Dr. Seuss, was a wonderful town with pink, orange and yellow Truffula trees. There were dozens of green, lush hills. A beautiful river, crystal clear with fish of every kind.

The mayor of the town, Mr. Chatterbox, wore a long hat, colored white and red just like the cat in the hat. He loved to boast about how good he looked in the hat.

The Mayor's assistant, Mr. Green, was the 'Lorax' of the town. He had yellow shaggy eyebrows and a thick yellow moustache that covered half his face. Mr. Green wore an orange coat, orange sweater, orange pants and orange socks and looked just like the Lorax.

Everyone loved Seussville, everyone except Teensy-Weensy. Teensy-Weensy was a girl far too small and scrawny for her age. She went to Swomee Swans School and the students would call her 'Teensy- Weensy Spider'.

One afternoon, when Teensy-Weensy was walking back home, some kids were passing by and one of them giggled, "Oh look who it is, Teensy-Weensy spider! HaHaHa!" and the others chorused, "Teensy-Weensy spider! Teensy-Weensy spider!" and blew raspberries at her.

Teensy-Weensy glared at the rude kids, but was too scared to retort. Teensy-Weensy ran away from the cheeky kids and in her hurry accidentally bumped into.....GRUMPY LUMPY!!!

Grumpy Lumpy, was a horrid, creepy person who looked like a bag of bones. He never smiled, nor laughed. He was literally the Grinch himself!

However, unlike the Grinch, it seemed that Grumpy Lumpy would never change for the better.

Now back to the story, when Teensy- Weensy hit Grumpy's back, he turned around and yelled with a cracking voice, "Who hit me? Show yourself you cheeky worm!" he grunted, shouted, "Who-" but stopped as he looked down at Teensy-

Weensy and said, "You seem tttiiiinnnyy." Teensy-Weensy froze, her knees shaking and palms sweating "Why did I have to bump into the worst person in town," she thought.

She replied stammering, "I-I k-k- know I-I'm short," she continued, "I-I'm really s-s-sorry Mr. Grumpy."

Grumpy-Lumpy barked, "Then grow TALLER!! AND GET OUT OF MY SIGHT YOU LITTLE PEST!" Teensy-Weensy didn't have to be told twice, she ran away as fast as her little feet could carry her.

As Teensy-weensy neared her home, she slowed down. Her home was beautiful with pretty tiles and enormous yellow and orange Truffula trees surrounding it.

The little girl opened the door, and saw her grandmother busy staring at the T.V., with wide eyes. Grandma looked up from the T.V and smiled at Teensy-weensy,

"Hello Teensy-Weensy, had a good day?" and then looked back at the T.V. Teensy-Weensy responded, "Terrible! kids kept calling me Teensy-Weensy spider and I accidentally bumped into Mr. Grumpy-Lumpy," Grandma shocked, put the T.V off and exclaimed, "Oh! That's bad."

"I know right, Grandma, I try so hard to fit in, but that never seems to work out."

"Then why try to fit in when you were born to stand out?"

"Sounds like a good piece of advice," thought Teensy-Weensy.

That was when Teensy-Weensy changed the topic and asked, "Grandma, what were you watching?"

The old lady replied, "You know the Suess Museum, right?" Teensy-Weensy nodded, grandma continued, "The very first copy of the Lorax was stolen and it is worth millions! Turns out there have been other robberies in town, the original hat that the 'cat in the hat' wore was also stolen and so much more was stolen from the museum. There are guards every night standing around the museum but they never seem to be able to catch this skilled thief."

Teensy-Weensy now had eyes as big as saucers and her mouth was wide open. She ran to her room and closed the door. She thought,"Hmmm... I think I can catch this thief...I'm so small no one will even notice I'm near the museum."

Teensy- Weensy packed up her bag,she carried a torch and a heavy ball. That night, she snuck out of her house and cycled to the museum, in the moonlight. As Teensy-Weensy neared the museum, she saw the guards standing around the museum. She hid her cycle and treaded on the grass when suddenly.... she found herself falling down a dug-up tunnel. "AAAAARRRRGGGGGGHHHH," she yelled.

She fell hard and looked up, the hole was narrow, enough only for someone as thin as her to go through. She was walking towards the end of the tunnel when she hit her head on something hard. She looked up and hit the hard thing on top of her. It surprisingly moved, she pushed it and realized it was a loose tile maybe one loosened by the thief to enter... the Seuss Museum.

She entered the museum and admired everything around, when suddenly she saw the... THIEF!

He was happily holding the very pen Dr. Seuss used to write with. Teensy-Weensy put up a brave act and shouted, "Hey thief, put down that pen right this instant."

The thief looked at the little girl and yelled, "Who are you?" and Teensy-Weensy put her torch on and it hit the thief, he screamed, "OWWWWWW...my eyes...put it away....wait a minute you're that girl who bumped into me the other day... come here you little MAGGOT!"

But, Teensy-Weensy wouldn't, instead she took out her ball and threw it at the thief's foot. As he yelled in agony, Teensy-Weensy exclaimed, "Mr. Grumpy, you thief!"

The guards who were wondering what the commotion was, saw Seuss' pen on the floor. Shocked, their eyes bounced between Teensy-Weensy and Mr. Grumpy. Teensy- Weensy yelled in exasperation, "Guards, Mr. Grumpy is the thief."

The next day, Mr. Chatterbox congratulated her while the citizens of Seussville cheered. Mr. Green planted a Truffula tree in her honour. Teensy-Weensy ecstatically thought, "WHY FIT IN WHEN YOU WERE BORN TO STAND OUT!"

Chatterbox questioned, "Don't I just look splendid in my hat?"

"Mr. Chatterbox!!"

"What?! I need to know I look good."

The Story of Adam and Amir

by Mallawa Arachchige Gagana Wathsanda Perera

GEORGE AND HARROLD WERE USUALLY RESPONSIBLE KIDS. WHENEVER ANYTHING BAD HAPPENED, GEORGE AND AROLD WERE USUALLY RESPONSIBLE.

In a delightful Island, with light blue sky and marshy lands surrounded by mountains, there lived two siblings called Adam and Amir. They lived with their parents and neighbors. Even though they were very clever, they loved mischiefs. Every day they played together and had wonderful time.

Adam and Amir had a secret place for them to plan how to being bad and make fun of others.

It was their school holidays. One evening when the sun was setting they heard Amir's dad talking with someone behind the bushes. After a while they came to know a visitor is coming to their home for a stay. Adam and Amir ran to the tree house where they can do all plans without others interruption.

Amir said, "Adam, this is a great chance for us to have fun."

"Oh yes Amir, we can scare him with scary wolf sound when he sleep at night. Also make a deep wide hole in the garden full with water and a carpet on top and cover the carpet with grass and let him fall in to it," Adam said.

"We will do that tomorrow when he's leaving for his morning walk," Amir said.

Adam said, "Amir, you go get the radio and I will get a carpet, spade and water".

Next, they hid everything in the tree house. It was night time Amir's dad and the visitor arrived by the car. They entered the house and Amir's mom and sister served the dinner to Mr. Brayan, the visitor. They had a joyful gathering after a long busy day. After few hours everyone got ready to sleep but no one knew Adam and Amir is still awake in the tree house. Adam said, "Give me the radio please," Amir gave it to Adam.

They searched for scary wolf sounds and went to the house with the radio hid inside the pocket. Adam tip-toed in to the visitor's bed room and played the wolf sound and ran away to the tree house. They heard Mr. Brayan walk up and screamed.

Two boys talked about their second plan and then Adam whispered, "Amir, Let's go and dig a hole in the garden." Then they both dig the hole in the middle of the garden near the walking lawn behind the mango tree. They completed their plan as they discussed before going to bed.

In the early morning when the Mr. Brayan was drinking morning tea, Amir went secretly to fill the water in to the hole and cover it with the carpet. Mr. Brayan set off for his morning walk. He was admiring the nature and the chirping of the birds. Adam and Amir were hiding behind the bushes and watching him. When Mr. Brayan came back from his lovely journey, he suddenly fell into the whole Adam and Amir dig last night.

Mr. Brayan started shouting, Adam and Amir went laughing inside the tree house.

Amir's mom rushed in to the garden and Mr. Brayan again shouted, "Who dig this hole here?"

Amir's mom called Adam and Amir. They came to the garden. Their father also came rushing in to the garden and asked, "What happened here?"

Mom said, "Mr Brayan fell down in to the deep hole, please hurry up and help him." Adam's dad helped him to come out from the hole.

"Do you even know who is Mr. Brayan?" said Adam's dad.

"Who is he dad?" Adam and Amir asked.

"This is your new teacher," his father replied angrily.

He again protested, "You've been naughty enough for whole month. Not only that, you also made your teacher to fall into the hole."

Amir and Adam got really scared and apologized to Mr. Brayan. "We are really sorry Mr. Brayan, please forgive us. Mom and Dad please excuse us, we never do this again."

Mr. Brayan said, "Oh, it's all fine. But never do it again to anyone. I am happy to meet you little champs."

Adam and Amir went to the room and talked how they were bad to others in this whole month and promised each other never to be bad again.

By Gaurika Gautam

"You're Mad, Bonkers, Completely Off Your Head. But I'll Tell You A Secret. All The Best People Are".

– Alice In Wonderland. Lewis Carroll.

As a child "Alice in Wonderland" reverberates with every child, especially girls. I would imagine myself running around in a beautiful fluffy frock, swirling in circles of joy and discovery. Every time, I saw darkness, I would step back but then be compelled to look again, can I see a monster? But then this temptation would tell me, the portal to the other world lies there. Maybe today is my lucky day, I will experience life as Alice did. And then, I hear my mother calling my name, what's keeping me back.

I agree, while you are reading this, you are thinking, this is just what I used to do. Don't fret, It's the story of every imaginative child. My thoughts always lost, wandering around fiction, trying to find another end to that story. What if?

These amazing stories get the creative juices of my brain flowing and literature is what keeps the hope of tomorrow flickering.

This quote by Lewis Carroll always gets me excited, it makes me confident, ready to chart out a new path. Alice always makes me fearless and teaches me to take on challenges. For, I am learning, it is the tough moments in life which shape our destiny and form our personality.

I know, we all have our fears and insecurities, big or small, important or not. The best is to face them and beat them. The warrior with a strategy emerges victorious. And now I understand what my father means when he says, "You don't fight every battle, choose them."

"I'll tell you a secret,"this sentence so craft fully worded by Lewis Carroll has always sparked the curiosity and adventure in me. It attracts me to explore this voyage of mystery. It implores me to go where no one has gone before. It's the joy of madness, sheer magic of willingness to acquire new things in life, be it skills, friends, honors, love, fame, success, anything. These thoughts guided me to ace my fear of darkness. Fear of darkness, is that even a fear? For a small child yes, certainly. It can catch the lights out of me. It freezes me. As if I am stuck in time. A demon is standing right there to catch me and throw me to infinity to be lost forever. Every dark space actually would get my thinking cap on, and a new story emerges every single time. Though, the story is always a little scary, yes, with a different theme and me standing at the end of the tunnel in the light. I made it. I discovered it as a novel way to hone my imagination skills and finding words to the humor lost in it. I realized with time, I was getting better at formulating phrases to get the point across. The churning feeling inside me would get a cloak on and I would steal the spotlight as the superhero. But my best friend, as we all know it by the name of shyness, will always sticks to me and I just can't get to dusting it off me. No worries I thought, I will write for myself. This is one thing I did for myself. It's my secret, my force reckoning me to novel spaces. I have to just follow Alice and go on without looking back. All strings unattached, I might appear alone but when I turn back, I see my family, my friends, my mentors smiling at me repurposing their belief in me.

This is my story of how I am improving at it. I know I have miles to go but it's a life long journey. Every day is a unique learning. Every encounter is like a new story, a new adventure. Our imaginations could be limitless. When I was a little younger, I used to imagine people having horns on their head and as I grow up, I find, it gives a unique perspective. I realize it changes with the kind of energy that surrounds us. Like, when I am at my swimming training, I sometimes imagine all the sea creatures swimming around me, and I would often think the water could understand what I am saying. I am a water diva and water is my second skin. I often even think of me having superpowers and saving the world. Like Dr. Strange!! I could create this imaginary circle with my hands and save the day !

But being Alice is always the fun part. Because this role is such a captivating one. Nothing scares me anymore. I am ready for wonderland. I can totally relate to the deep meaning of why being mad, being bonkers and being completely off our heads is the best thing. The best people bring about a change, a chain reaction, they walk the untrodden path and discover new frontiers.

Till, I reach the shining beam... see you there.

"Numbing the pain for a while will only make it feel worsen when you finally feel it."

— J. K. Rowling, Harry Potter And The Goblet Of Fire

Sunken Stasis

by Tamanna Shibu

We stood in our kitchen. Yellow rays of light shining down on us, he faced the sink and I the stove. Our backs facing each other. The conversation hung like an invisible damp cloud that dimmed the yellow light. There were murmurs and noises I couldn't decipher.

He then asks me to fetch him a pan from the cabinet. And so I slide my hand past the air lazily and I resume, tired, bending and reaching out to the cabinet. Head crooked I stare at it, squinting. A black hole and its event horizon. I stay, refusing to speak, hand covering my throat.

Time sweeps past me, I reach my hand into it. And it's empty, a void. I repeatedly try to dig deep into my black-hole-cabinet. Frantic and Frivolous. Regret trickles past my cheeks and down my shoulders. Little streams until I cry myself a river. I watch them flow around my legs and feet. Twirling and swerving, around the rim of white dress, turning it damp and then pale grey.

I panic while my back aches against the weight of his gaze and restlessness. One hand against the door of the cabinet for support and the other disappearing into the void. I continue to search for the pan in nothingness, in fear and perhaps crying.

He begins to yell and screech. I yell and look above and below, trying to get up but the hole draws me in with my water and misery. I yelp. But it's quiet, my excavation oblivious to everyone else I suppose. My body is a pathetic pile like a heap on the floor. And I rummage hopelessly. I peer into the nothingness and my hands tremble.

The void keeps growing, the water level rises and I can not stop crying. His voice stifles my ears. It's cold, I begin to shiver. I watch as the hole grows faster, and I realize water climbing up my waist. It's clear cold blue in the kitchen all around. Water is stuck in the kitchen, but flows only into the hole.

'It's a pan,' he whispers, his voice slithering past the air.

'I'm trying, it's not there, I'm telling you it's not there."

'IT'S A PAN!' he repeats, impatient.

'Look! Please, I beg you,' I wail. He doesn't turn.

I rampantly try digging deeper and faster, nothing. My white dress now grey, swells and shrinks, with every tear drop. I keep gnawing at its emptiness. The yellow hue subdues into blue, and I taste the water and it gushes into my mouth.

Why didn't I stop the void from growing? I think.

It fills my nostrils and burns my eyes.

He vanishes. Nor can I hear demands or commands, every voice and sound sink, muffled into a loud piercing hum. Huddled at the bottom, the water and void both still, I resign. I don't fight it anymore. I don't escape. I let it go, I forget about him and the pan. I nudge my way past into the void. Into the blackness and emptiness. One foot and one hand at a time. Awaiting to be taken away, I don't close my eyes. I render to it. I leave everything behind; it's serene and stagnant. And I glare into it.

Hope

by Mir Faraz

Exhausted, Sultan rested his head on the springy turf of dewy grass. Despite himself, his gaze was fixated on the horizon in the vain hope that he would see one of his kind. He had been alone for too long.

Sultan was a White Rhinoceros- the last of his species alive on the planet. The very last. After he was gone, White Rhinoceroses would be added to the ever-growing list of extinct species.

Every year more than 10,000 species of animals go extinct. Sultan's species had endured the same fate because of two reasons – destruction of their habitat due to human activities and poaching of Rhinos to obtain their horns which were sold for a handsome fortune.

Sultan had seen his helpless family members and friends being captured and killed for their horns. He never really understood what good the horns were to the humans anyway.

Sultan was brought to the Masai Mara conservation park in Kenya after his mother became a victim of the "horn takers". He was just two years old at that time. Days had morphed into years and now he was forty-six. It was a good life he had lived. He did not like to think otherwise. He had been luckier than the rest. The humans at the park were his friends and took the best care of him. There were armed guards with him round the clock, protecting him like the national treasure that he was considered to be. The last white rhinoceros.

Lately, Sultan had not been keeping very well. His gait was slower, and his breathing strained. He had lived a long life, but it was time now. He could feel it.

One of the guards who had been guarding Sultan since a very young age bent down and gently stroked Sultan's ears and whispered with a quiver in his voice-

"You're braver and stronger than you could ever know, old friend. I only wish you could have had the life you deserved. You and all those who lived before you. You belong to the wild – free; not here with us guarding you with guns. Rest now, dear one. Remember, we'll love you forever..."

Sultan looked up, his old eyes full of gratitude and unadulterated love for everyone who had devoted their entire lives to him. He wondered why all humans couldn't be like the people standing before him, "Perhaps in another world, another lifetime, we'll all coexist together."

Sultan's eyelids drooped closed. And then, almost instantly, he opened his eyes again. He looked around. No longer was he within the confines of the park. He was in a land which seemed like it was floating in the air. Sultan took a deep breath. The air felt fresh and pristine. He looked around in wonder and then a flickering movement in the distance caught his eye. Sultan turned, and saw, to his very surprise, a herd of animals coming towards him. As they came closer, Sultan realized what they were Rhinos! He said out loud, "White Rhinos! Like me!"

Sultan galloped towards the White Rhinos and noticed that all feelings of weakness had left him since he arrived there; his joints didn't hurt anymore and his breath didn't come in sputters. He felt like he had been reborn. Sultan stopped in front of the Rhinos, and the Rhino leading the group gracefully stepped forward.

Sultan thought she looked strangely familiar. And then she spoke. Just one word, "Sultan?" That quivering voice revived a distant memory in Sultan's mind. He spoke, his own voice choked, "Mother?"

The beautiful Rhinoceros smiled, "It's been so long, Sultan!" she said, "Look how grown up you are!"

Sultan then asked the question that had been tickling his brain for a while now, "Am I... in Heaven?" Happy tears welled in his eyes, as he knew what the answer would be.

"Yes, Sultan, you are," his mother said, "And now we can be together forever and ever!"

As Sultan nuzzled against his mother, he said a silent prayer that the world would be kinder to all lifeforms. He hoped that one day the world would be a better place- a place where every life would matter.

Turbulence

by Sara Kulkarni

*"I am not afraid of storms, for I am learning
how to sail my ship"* –

Little Women by Louisa May Alcott.

An island of a ship, about to perish in a tidal wave
of water during an eternal storm.

The ship's captain has been conquered by the
salty liquid, or so it seems.

An oasis of gold in an algae - filled ocean, a
reservoir of opportunities,

Is disappearing swiftly.

My mind is like the ocean,

but not the one written about in literature
regarding searching for some gratified true

meaning. Rather, it appears to be akin to the rancid or grotesque depictions of deep sea life.

Ridden by weird forms of creatures and unusual flora.

The ship struggles to stay afloat.

The crew jumps overboard survived by the hopes of swimming to a new existence. However, the ship remains.

Too heavy to flee, too adamant to stay.

Among the gloomy and faraway depths of my sea, are colours. Hidden. Schools of clownfish swim among the tangled coral,

their bright orange juxtaposing the deranged blue hues.

The powerless but moving tiny speck of white and brown is now determined to move against the endless cobalt.

Though lonely and irrelevant to the complexities of the world as a speck of sand on the shore, the ship exhibits a vehement desire –

To evolve. To explore. To last.

Suddenly, the seaweed contaminating the caverns of my psyche began to float away like littered trash bags in the ocean.

The light from up above permeates the liquid with a boundless yet bountiful glow.

After what feels like years, the faint warmth of dawn light has reached every nook and cranny of this neglected sea.

I am no longer scared of choking on the mundane. I am no longer afraid of drowning in the ocean. For now, the ship is free. Tired. But free.

Even though there was comfort in attaining solitude, By giving in to the tide -

I am a phoenix of the water.

Risen from the sawdust of my past life, Inescapably,

The ship and I are one.

Old Friends

by Mishal Faraz

"Quickly, Alyssa!" my mother calls out in a strangled yell. I sprint desperately towards her and grab her outstretched hand, but then a loud "squawk" coming from my room makes me let go of it.

"Alyssa, no!" my mother cries, running after me. I dash across the corridor with one arm over my head to shield myself from the rubble descending from the ceiling. Bursting through the door, I frantically scan the room. Spotting the bright white cage, I swiftly pick it up and run.

Exiting the building, I look around in horror. Chaos reigns around me – people running, children crying, houses crumbling. Scattered flames eerily light up the terrified expressions on people's faces.

In front of me, my mother comes to a halt. Panic in her eyes, her hands quivering, she reaches down and pulls open the door to our air-raid shelter. She takes my hand, guiding me as I gingerly find my footing in the looming blackness below, still holding on to the cage.

I hear a scratch as my mother lights a candle. Set on an upturned fruit crate in the centre of the cramped room, the candle glows feebly.

"Try to get some sleep, Alyssa," my mother says, "We leave in the morning. There is some food and water, but not much."

"Yes, Mama," I squeak quietly, rummaging through our sparse resources, "And is there birdseed too?" I ask.

"Yes, of course, dear" my mother replies, pointing. I grab the bag right away, and then crawl towards the birdcage. I rip open the bag and refill the food container.

He doesn't understand the concept of rationing food, I think resolutely. He shouldn't have to starve and suffer. I gently drag the cage closer to me, looking at the beautiful bird inside.

My Smokey. He was a majestic parrot, with an even larger personality and voice. His steel grey plumage was smooth and glistening, ending in a magnificent tail of blue and crimson. I had had him since he was a little chick, when he could fit into the palm of my hand. I would spend hours playing with him and teaching him words to repeat.

I open the cage door and hold out my hand. As usual, he affectionately nips my finger with his beak before hopping up with an elegant flutter and settling himself on his spot on my shoulder.

"Bedtime, bedtime," he squawks. He then proceeds to tuck his head under his wing and doze off to sleep. Shutting my eyes, I lean back against the hard wall.

The next morning the candle lies on the floor, shrunken and extinguished, and Smokey is back in his cage.

"Moooorning!" he caws shrilly, and I reach through the still open door and pet him on his head.

"Oh good, Alyssa, you're awake," my mother says, "come on, we need to go."

She slings the tiny rucksack around her shoulders and I take Smokey's cage. I gasp as I step outside.

Everything is gone. All the buildings reduced to rubble. I barely have time to mourn the loss of my home and village as my mother leads me to a throng of people some distance away.

"Where are we going, Mama?" I whisper.

"It's not safe here anymore, Alyssa," my mother whispers back, "we need to leave the country."

My heart stops. Where would we go? Will we be refugees? I'm absolutely petrified, but I just continue to walk.

The walk seems to go on for hours. The merciless sun scorches my neck, my arms ache from carrying Smokey for so long, and my cheap sandals do nothing to shield me from the painful, rocky terrain.

We arrive at what looks like a small, rudimentary airport. A man wearing a volunteer jacket jogs towards us.

"Come on, everyone!" he yells, "This is the last plane flying out today!"

I've never seen an airplane up close before, and it's bigger than I could have possibly imagined. I'm just about to climb the steps when he grabs me by the arm.

"Excuse me, miss, but you can't take that parrot in here," he says.

"I-, oh," I stutter, "I'm sorry, I don't understand."

The volunteer sighed, "We're not taking animals."

He holds out his hands for the cage, and my mother steps in, "Please, sir, he won't take up much space."

"I'm sorry," he says firmly, "that's my final word."

Tears start streaming down my face. How could I give my Smokey away? He would be so confused and scared. Who will take care of him? The man tries to take the cage from me, and I hold on to it with all my might, but just can't compete with his strength. Blinded by my tears, I lunge forward to take the cage back but my mother holds me back. "There's nothing we can do, Alyssa. We don't want to get into trouble," she spoke, her voice trembling.

And with that, I do the hardest thing I've ever done, and leave my precious Smokey behind. I take one last glance at him. His intelligent, bright yellow eyes were wide and sceptical now as he looked at me as if demanding answers.

"Alyssa, Alyssa!" he squawks as tears blur my vision and the world fades away.

***

It's been one year since I fled my home. I live in a new country with my mother. We have been given a small but comfortable house. I even go to school. Life somewhat has a normalcy to it.

But I miss Smokey every day. I've replayed that fateful day in my head endlessly. Why hadn't I been more adamant to keep him? But strangely enough, although thoughts rage through my mind, I don't talk about Smokey, ever. I find it easier to numb the pain. My mother disagrees. She says that numbing the pain only makes it feel worse when you finally feel it. She keeps trying to get me to talk about him, to reminisce about his shenanigans. She's even suggested getting a new pet parrot to open my heart to another animal. But no other bird can replace Smokey.

Suddenly, the doorbell rings, jolting me out of my thoughts. It's my mother with a huge crate.

"Alyssa!" she beams, "I've got a surprise for you!"

She sets the crate down in the living room. It's got air holes in it. I immediately know what's inside.

"Mama," I sigh despondently, "I don't want a new pet."

"But don't you want to have a look?" she replies, a strange twinkling in her eye.

"I got a call from an NGO a few days back," she continues, still smiling. "They provide shelter for animals who are separated from their owners in warzones. They protect these animals, give them a home and then try to reunite these pets with their families."

My breath is caught in my throat as I comprehend what my mother meant. I open the cart frantically as my heart struggles to keep its pace.

There he was! The cage was different, but it was him alright!

"Smokey!" I exclaim. To my great exhilaration, he recognizes me! He starts flapping his wings in delight, and even though I know it's not physically possible, he almost seems to be smiling. I open the cage door hurriedly, and he flies out immediately and settles himself on my shoulder. It's as if not even a day has passed.

"Alyssa, Alyssa!" he squawks.

Smokey nuzzles his head against mine, and I couldn't tell who was happier right now.

"Welcome home, old friend," I whisper as I feel my heart becoming whole again.

Arthur and Vanilla

by Rishika Bajaj

Huuuizzz! Swaying to and fro in the soothing breeze were lush green leaves that fell into the beautiful Lanka River.

The smell of the damp muddy soil near the river was suffocating the surroundings. Vanilla – a majestic owl - was perched on the apple tree with scrumptious fruit and smooth leaves.

One day, gazing through the thick bushes of sharp pines, Arthur noticed Vanilla's shimmering eyes. Arthur lifted his head high and sprinted across the shrubs, water pools, springs, and rose gardens.

Within a fraction of second Vanilla halted and bowed graciously majesty and said, "Evening majesty some birds to see us race as I soar the skies as the swift princess and you claim to be the fastest in the land," suggested Vanilla.

Arthur was filled with pride and he brimmed with confidence that he would be crowned the champion of speed. He perceived that he would certainly be victorious over Vanilla.

Hence, he exclaimed, "Of course! I can have the council make a long and tiring race that can final who is the king of speed."

"Or Queen," Vanilla added.

As the race started, the sun was setting and the forest was dark and with unknown traps and challenges that lay ahead. Bundru, the umpire blew the whistle and the two animals set out. At first, Arthur was ahead while Vanilla was not seen anywhere in sight. Interestingly, Arthur slowed down once he commenced the first task.

Arthur had not realized that Vanilla could fly over all the traps. Then, he presumed that she got lost. The crowd waited eagerly to see who was going to lose their title a majestic owl or a mighty king. himself. On the other hand, Vanilla was on top of her game.

There was a broken bridge on top of a pool with wild alligators. Suddenly, Arthur saw a blinding light and could sense a wonderful fragrance. He followed the light and glimpsed an enormous mansion that he had never seen before. He was perplexed. Arthur was exhausted and he yearned for some nice leisure time in the mansion. Meanwhile, he determined to fix the broken bridge with his sharpened skills. And so, he went in.

A short time later, he woke up and realized that he was behind the plan. So, he began to explore the mansion to identify an object that he could use as a bridge.

After a while, he saw a rugged chess board and heaved it as a bridge. He quickly dashed across the path as he knew that Vanilla was far ahead. It took him a while to heave it to the lake. Then, he gathered momentum and paced across the board. SPLASH! Arthur went deep into the pool.

Lights! Camera! Action!

The splash woke up the alligators. They surrounded Arthur with their spear-like teeth ready to pounce on him. An old alligator with dark green skin and a sharp texture bit Arthur and he was yelping. All the animals of the Azura Forest came to witness the one who had fallen for the trap.

Arthur yelped for help though none of the animals came forward to help him, they thought it was unfair that they would help him it would be cheating.

So Bundru the umpire said, "I am sorry your megacity we shan't help you it is against the rules of the Race," And saying this, Bundru and the other animals went off to the finish line waiting to see who would come first.

After a bit of struggle, Arthur managed to reach land, luckily, he had come to the shore that led to the part of the race track, he ran a few miles until he needed water as his throat was dry because of the continuous running. He knew there was a stream because of the sound of water gurgling and took some sips of water. He walked as slow as a snail and did not even think about the race. As soon as he had drunk water, he was energized and ready to run. He ran like the wind over the mountains and reached the next trap, there was a high fence towering high about the trees and not even Vanilla could fly over it.

Vanilla had been flying tirelessly while Arthur had been resting. She was also above Arthur near the fence. Suddenly, a string caught her sharp eye. As she flew closer, the hearts of the other animals raced to see if Vanilla could find a way to pass through the obstacle. The string was replacing a part of the wire as it was gone. So, Vanilla thought it was the weakest part of the bar. She was quick as light to cut open the string. She also left a huge hole in the bar, so she quickly flew, leaving Arthur behind.

Arthur who was still trying to find a way past the bar had not noticed vanilla but had noticed the big hole. He paced a few meters back and after a few attempts, he jumped through the hole to the other side of the fence.

To his despair, Vanilla dashed through the finish line and the next day was crowned the queen of speed.

All You Have to do is Believe

by Mazen Hameed

In a quiet village where everything looked the same and everyone knew each other, there was a little boy called Dan who lived with his dad Peter. They lived very ordinary lives and the chance of anything exciting or new happening to them in their lifetime was slim. Peter was a soldier like most men in the village. Due to his injury, he was no longer active in service, and this made him very unhappy and unpleasant. Most people steered clear of him. Peter forced his unaccomplished dreams onto his son and pushed him towards military life without considering that maybe this was not Dan's calling. Dan wanted to be an artist and express his thoughts and feelings in painting. He oozed creativity and saw the world as his canvas. Dan's favorite thing to do was to daydream where his imagination took over and there was no space for negativity or unhappiness. Not much was known about Dan's mother or any other family. Peter was Dan's only family and what a sad life that was – his father had a strict routine for him that left little time for Dan's art and even lesser joy in the poor boy's life.

Days rolled into weeks and weeks rolled into years. On an ordinary Sunday, Peter and Dan had returned from church and had taken their normal place at the breakfast table. Peter was reading the newspaper while Dan was quietly munching on his toast.

Peter tutted with disdain, "Nonsense!" he grumbled.

Interest piqued, Dan snuck a quick look at the newspaper. The article had Dan in utter disbelief. "A MIRROR THAT SHOWS YOUR FUTURE HAS BEEN FOUND!" screamed the headline.

Dan gasped in amazement. This magical mirror would be toured across Europe and to Dan's luck the nomadic exhibition was making its way to their village the following week! Right then Dan decided he must see this enchanted invention. He had to know what was his destiny – would he be a soldier like his father, or would he be able to live out his dream of becoming an artist?

It turns out his school had planned to take all the children to the moving museum. The next few days Dan spent in agony. He counted the minutes until the day of the excursion arrived.

It was finally D-Day! Dan could barely contain his excitement. Seeking clarity on their future, the children joined the long, snake-like line by dozens to the entrance of the museum. Curiosity was building up. The suspense was palpable. After what felt like an eternity it was finally Dan's turn and he was trembling with anticipation...

Flashbacks of his childhood whizzed through his mind. Fear of ending up like his father took over his brain. Endless hours doing a monotonous job that brought him no joy sent shivers down his spine. And then Dan imagined the colors of his easel. Endless possibilities. Immeasurable joy from being the master of his own life. What would the mirror show him? Eyes closed tight, Dan held his breath and tried to calm his heartbeat.

Slowly, Dan opened his eyes and what lay in front of him was pure magic! He saw brightness and wonder - a world filled with hope and happiness everywhere. There was love and laughter and joy. With a great sigh of relief, Dan took one last look at the magic that lay in front of him and truly believed that anything was possible for him.

"A little magic can take you a long way."

Colourful Substitutes

by Sanjana Jove

The sunrise brings renewed uneasiness,

Brown birds perform a plaintive song,

I swallow colourful capsules

with a snowball's chance in hell,

I'm incredibly tired already.

I eat less with every spoon,

Each step so much harder than the first,

Mountains of melancholy

ride the elevator with me,

I'm incredibly tired already.

Then a yellow butterfly

finds its way into my city,

A paper aeroplane whizzes past me,

Green plums fall on my way to work,

Dandelions rest on my shoulders,

The café waiter offers to reheat my untouched coffee,

He knows things are difficult right now.

Today the birds don't sing the same tune,

The sunrise simply a familiar glow.

My heart a little happier,

As I ride the elevator alone.

The Cat Who Cried Wolf

by Aanvi Gupta

In a far away land called Ephedia stood Xeris High where the kids of fairy-tale characters studied. There lived a girl named Cerise Hood, daughter of red riding hood. Cerise was racing her wolf called Fang in the Evergreen forest and Cerise won. Fang licked Cerise's face and pushed down her hood and saw her wolf ears, hoping nobody saw, Cerise put it back on and then she heard a voice. It was Kitty Cheshire, daughter of the Cheshire Cat.

"You beat that wolf in a race ! How do you do it?" cried Kitty.

"You can't tell anyone about this Kitty," replied Cerise in panic.

Just then Raven came, she was the daughter of the evil queen but Raven had a good heart, she did not want to follow in her mom's footsteps.

Raven said, "Cerise?"

Without turning, she growled like a wolf at her and stopped after she turned. "Do you want to talk about it?" asked Raven nicely.

Cerise sighed and said, "I guess .... it would be nice to talk to someone about it." Then she opened her necklace. It was her family.

Raven gaped and cried, "Your mom, Red Riding Hood, married The Big Bad Wolf! Don't worry, your secret is safe with me. Cerise smiled at her. The next day, Coach Gingerbread made an announcement about the BookBall Competition and so the training started after the interruption made by Apple White, Daughter of Snow White.

She told everyone, "I, Apple White, announce that Legacy day will be scheduled next Thursday. Thank you."

The next day, BookBall training began just then Tiny a giant came and told that they are against the students of Beanstalk high. Daring, Charming, the eldest son of Prince Charming told Tiny, "How hard can it be to beat small beans from beanstalk high."

Then Sparrow Hood, son of Robin Hood said, "Giants study at Beanstalk high not beans."

"Then we are in a lot of trouble aren't we?" replied Daring.

A couple of minutes later, Cerise came and asked if she can join the boys team for BookBall but Daring said, "Damsels in Distress are for catching not for running."

Cerise growled and stomped away but she joined anyway. The next day running practice started and Kitty was acting weird. Coach Gingerbread blew the whistle. Kitty opened a box and a deer jumped out of it and Cerise's behavior changed like a wolf and then she started chasing it, she ran faster than everyone. Suddenly, the deer jumped back inside the box.

"So Cerise," started Kitty in a sing-song voice as Cerise clutched her hood, "do you have anything to tell us?"

Cerise was speechless just then Raven said, "Oh wow! I can't believe that the running spell I casted on your sneakers worked."

"What?" asked Kitty in confusion.

"Thanks Raven," thanked Cerise.

The next day it was LEGACY DAY when the kids of the fairy tale characters sign the story book of legends to become just like their parents.

"I am Apple White, daughter of Snow White and I pledge to be the next queen of Ephedia," said Apple.

All eyes were on raven as she said, "I am Raven, Queen daughter of the Evil Queen and I pledge... I am Raven Queen and I want to write my own destiny, my happily ever after starts now."

Cedar Wood, daughter of Pinocchio and Maddie (Madeline Hatter), daughter of the Mad Hatter runs up to her. "Raven, the book is a fake. This is not the story book of legends it's just a book of fairy tales," cried Cedar.

"What?" shouted Maddie. "That is just MAD."

"Then where is the real story book of legends," exclaimed Briar Beauty, daughter of Sleeping Beauty.

"We have to find the real story book of legends," replied C.A Cupid, adopted daughter of Eros. "Then were coming too," said Apple and Ashlyn Ella, Daughter of Cinderella and Blondie Locks, daughter of GoldiLocks and so Raven, Briar, Apple, Ashlyn, Maddie, Blondie, Cupid, Cedar and

Cerise had set of to find the real story book of legends. The girls had no idea where to go until Farrah Gracelyn Goodfairy came and asked politely, "Do you guys need any help?"

Ashlyn replied, "Umm... can you tell us where is the story book of legends with your magic?"

"It's on the shelf in the library with Headmaster Grimm," Farrah replied.

"No, the real one," said Ashlyn.

"Oh it is in the BLOODHILL FOREST," said Farrah.

The girls set of to Bloodhill forest, on the other hand the book ball champions from Xeris high were in the lead. In Bloodhill Forest, the story book of legends was guarded by a blood sucking vampire named Godrick Hallows, and a flesh eating werewolf named Moonie Moonlight when they reached the fort Raven, found the story book of legends and was thinking this way too easy then she turned back face to face with Godrick and Moonie.

Raven tried her best to defeat them but they were unbeatable then Apple shouted, "The only way to beat them is to work as a team," and so Apple and all the other girls worked together side to side.

Then Godrick started making fun of Cerise's wolf ears and that had made her weak, she had never felt like this before. Then Cupid, Blondie and Maddie cheered her up while fighting Moonie together. Suddenly, she felt more confident than ever. The scores was 50 and 100 to Xeris High because Hopper Croakington II had found that giants little toe fingers are ticklish and the girls had made it back with the story book of legends just in time for the victory party.

A Shining Star

by Macayla Louise Hong

Drystan Raine Smythe, a lovely person, my closest friend, like a brother to me. Both our families referred to him as a Shining Star in a dark cloud because of his positivity. He is the life of the party, He always cheers people up when they are down and supported them. He never once got mad or sad by someone's negative actions. I remember him so well and he will be in my heart forever, but as times go by, I start to wonder.... how can a human never feel negative emotions? and here's why.

July 17, 2014, the day I learned the truth behind his actions. We had an argument about him being bullied and him never doing anything about it, he wasn't mad at all instead he was trying to calm me down, But I couldn't and I wouldn't just stand by and watch, I was fed up with him being bullied, he never told a teacher because he believes everybody deserves a "second chance". At the time I thought it was stupid. "YOU KNOW IF YOU WOULD ACTUALLY STAND UP FOR YOURSELF YOU WOULDN'T KEEP BEING CONTROLLED!" I said out of anger. "YOU NEED TO REALISE THE WORLD IS A TOUGH PLACE AND IF YOU CAN'T FIGHT BACK, YOU HAVE NO PLACE IN THIS WORLD!"

I was already sobbing at that point and that sentence made him stay silent, He started sniffling and then I knew what I said was a stupid idea, but I was just really upset. Then he looked up to me with tears in his eyes.

He started to become serious. "YOUR'E RIGHT, PEOPLE USE AND CONTROL ME BUT DO YOU REALLY WANT TO KNOW WHY I DON'T SAY ANYTHING?!" I stayed silent and nodded.

"Fine!" he choked on a sob. "I... the truth is I'm dying Mateo, I'm dying," he says that and then bursts into tears in front of my eyes. What have I done? I'm a monster."

"I-I'm sorry, I didn't know."

"It's fine," he said while wiping his tears quickly, "I did not want to tell you this, I have leukaemia and we found out when I was eight years old. My time to pass is coming soon and I'm getting quite sick now a days. The reason I'm always happy is because I want to give happiness to others that may not have it, I want to help as much people as I can, I'm never worried or in a rush so that I can have those precious moments of the time left before I go," he said.

I embraced him as hard as I could, and he did the same. The next few days, we were hanging out more, just spending time with each other, We valued the time We had left with each other. People tried bullying him, but I was always there to defend him and we would laugh about it for hours and from then on, I wanted to protect him, so I stayed by his side, we became inseparable.

No one could separate us. Not even our parents.

July 25, 2014, we were hanging out as usual and were talking about his illness. He said that he is more vulnerable to diseases as time passes then he stopped mid-sentence and collapsed to the ground, and I called 911 as fast as I could. He was rushed to the ICU in critical condition, they informed me that he suffered cardiac arrest, but I wasn't worried because I had faith in him, and prayed to God more than ten times but after a few hours, I lost hope, but God listened to my prayers because he recovered and I got a chance to touch and hug him. But after a few days, he suffered a stroke and he sadly passed away that day.

On the day of his funeral, I tried not to cry but I couldn't control my emotions. He told me never to be sad when this day comes but how can he expect me to hold back my tears?

On his grave, it was written Drystan Raine Smythe - May 23 1997- August 3 2014, "Our shining star".

I couldn't help but smile while crying because of the multiple memories rushing through my mind because of his title "A Shining Star". The memories gave me comfort and whenever I remembered his beautiful sunshine smile, it made my heart warm and my brain relaxed. My thoughts were soon interrupted when his mother came up to me sobbing - because of the loss of her son - with a letter in her hand. She handed it to me; it was from him.

The note read, To: Mateo, from your best friend Drystan.

I opened it and the letter read. Dear Mateo, if you're reading this letter, it means I'm gone. I'd like you to promise me a few things, it's like a small payment for helping you out throughout life. First of all, I would like you to be happy always and you should never hurry and never worry in life, value every moment with your family and friends because every second counts. I hope you can live life without me, but don't worry, I'm here watching over you and everyone. Love Drystan.

I was a mess and heartbroken after his funeral. Even when I smiled, despair filled my heart. I visited his grave daily and decided to try my best to move on and live by his words because that's what he wanted.

Now, I want you to learn something from this story about Drystan and I. I want you to always be happy, be with your family and friends. Don't worry about anything else in your life. Nothing can stop you except you. I mean, you'll never know when it's your time or others time to go. People may forget what we said but they will never forget how we made them feel. Always be a shining star to someone's life.

The Eternal Twins!

by Filza Ali

The Heart and Mind—
Exist
within the singular Flesh
aligned in the one, thick Flesh

Yet are they two worlds apart:
they quarrel,
dispute,
debate.

They make a person overwhelmed,
by thoughts and feelings,
making them go into a state of confusion.

The line is drawn
between right and wrong,
logically or emotionally.

A moment of confession,
is what Will impels.
To hold back,
is what the Mind suggests.

Sometimes it is the Heart,
that leads to a valley of fragrance
that you find a reason to smile,

or sometimes,

it's nought but the Mind
that brings an end to you being a vagrant,
hopeful of a life in epic style!

The Eternal Twins!

O Heart! Heart! Heart!

Know ye not?
Know ye not your Twin?

O Mind! Mind! Mind!
Know ye not?
Know ye not your Twin?

The Heart and Mind—
that work opposing;
where the Mind brings sense
and the Heart brings righteousness;
where they walk
hand in hand!

When something feels right but,
doesn't make sense,
trust your Heart
being wiser of the two.

Though the brain is rational,
and Heart known for its irrationality;
the Heart deduces,
what can't be seen,
can't be touched,
but only felt.

A broken soul:
it needs not a speaking Mind,
but a Heart that listens,
to be the Glue of the pieces.

Like shards of glass,
words hurt...
but the disparity of the two,
is so significant.

The computer will keep the inferior memories,
replaying the past over and over,

but the Heart-

BEHOLD!
It will Heal.
That's the power it holds.

Wish has limits,
but breaks them and marches forward.
The Mind being logical,
devalues morality onward,

but the Heart is aware
of what's key;
it will hide what resides inside
to not be diabolical-
scarring another for life.

Being Thoughtless or Heartless,
is common when working with one,
but deciding which ONE to be,
at what time,
is key—
to Life.

Tell me now,
Which is the key,
the Heart
or
the Mind?

A Beautiful Sight

by Rhianna Nicole

Magic. Oh what a beautiful sight
Tricking the admirers eyes with no such right,
It comes so beautiful, a magnificent view,
Not just a show but a special person with a
delicate glow.

It fills our hearts with such great joy,
However, when learning the truth that it was
just a toy,

anger and fear rummage through our brains,
that little moment of happiness suddenly goes
to vein.

He was my magic,
My beautiful sight,
But was it all a trick and all just a lie?
Or was it a forbidden wish that let out a cry?

We watched the sunset and the moon rise,

On a grassy hill with unbreakable ties,

I thought to myself, 'could this be it, my magic of life?',

Or was it just a constant rolling of a dice.

The stars began to show in the dark night sky,

But just for a few moments till they all said goodbye,

The magic of the sun, the moon, the stars,

They shined upon us but disappeared in just a few hours.

My magic, my beautiful sight,

Came so slow and left in a flight,

It Ceased to exist that delicate glow,

And my special person just moved with the flow

'Was it even real?' you may ask,

Or all just a trick that would never last,

The memories and laughs felt were all just magic,

As the sun rays settled about to vanish.

Magic is a moment that passes with time,

If only we could stop it, and enjoy its prime,

Everything comes to an end, even if you hold tight.

Magic, oh what a beautiful sight.

Firefly – A Monologue

by Selasie Ganku

"Promise me you'll remember, you are braver than you believe, stronger than you seem, smarter than you think."

— Winnie the Pooh by A. A. Milne

It's dark down here.

It always is.

It suits me, I think.

It hurts less.

Above, people go on with their lives. Smiling. Laughing. Making memories. And as always, from down below, I watch. Detached. Distant. Longing. As always, longing.

Some days are better than others. Some days are a little brighter. Some days I could almost reach out from my little, dark pit and feel the light. Other days, I fall into quicksand. Struggling to breathe, struggling to think, struggling to move. Darker and darker and darker until it's pitch black. The darkness becomes a vice, tighter and tighter and tighter until I might as well be dead.

I might as well be dead.

It's laughable.

If I were dead, I would be free from the dark. If I were dead, I would be at peace. Death is comfortable, death is certain. But, death. Death is pain. Death is suffering. Death is out of reach.

So, instead. I watch.

Light filters in from above, dull and foggy. Time passes without my notice as I watch the people up above. I look up and see a flash of light. Tiny and insignificant, but noticeable all the same.

Again. A flash of light. Again and again and again, tiny flashes of light coming closer and closer and closer. Might this be the end? It could be an angel, coming to save me from the ruins of my life.

Closer and closer and closer. I could reach out and touch it. Or I could leave it alone. I can't decide.

It lands on my face. I feel nothing. I stopped feeling long ago. It's an insect, I realise. A firefly. Small but bright. I sigh.

Imagine being a firefly. Carefree and blissful, flying through the air.

The little creature shoots around, filled with a childlike curiosity as it buzzes around me. Look at it, circling above me in spirals of light. Around and around and around, seemingly in place but all the while I see it getting higher and higher and moving closer to the light.

I want to be a firefly. Untethered and free, with wings to soar far, far away. I could be whoever I wanted to be, wherever I wanted to be. No one could stop me.

And I want to be free. I really want to be. I'm tired of being stuck in this dark, dark hole. Away from the world and all the opportunities it brings.

I can be like a firefly. Unburdened by the world. Flying; higher and higher and higher. I can stand and pull myself up.

I can leave the darkness behind.

I can refuse to be held back by my fears and insecurities.

I. Can. Fly.

A Glimmer Into Life

by Aran Mukhopadhyay

As she sat back in her chair with a book in her hand, Lily flipped to the page she had last been reading. She opened to Chapter 44 and started reading.

"Lovely weather so far. I don't know how long it will last, but I'm not afraid of storms, for I'm learning how to sail my ship."

A smile showed on Lily's lips as she remembered the lines that had inspired and motivated her to use the struggles of life as stepping stones to go farther in life. The quote, which had appeared in her life at an early age, had pushed her towards her goal. She leaned back in her chair and started thinking.......

Time went by like running water as the entrance exams neared and the pressure on Lily's shoulder increased day by day. She was locked up in her room, her only friends being the NCERT books and the serene moonlit nights. That day, she was with the Biology book, going through all the chapters, though she had revised it many times.

Lily was a studious child from India. She used to play badminton and football, and she could swim very well. But after class twelve, she was always found in her room with her nose buried in books. She was a passionate learner and knew that the road to being a doctor was difficult, but she was not afraid of hard work. But after nearly six months of being locked up in her house, she was starting to get depressed, and her only stress-relieving moments were those when she would walk in the endless fields of grass, staring at the shining moon with the occasional drizzle.

Lily's parents were perhaps her only real source of compassion and love. They were very supportive of Lily's wish, and they did everything to motivate and encourage her to follow her dream of becoming a doctor.

As the exam date neared, Lily felt more and more anxious. She knew that this was her chance to sail her ship, a chance to prove to the world that she would not be put down by hard work. She still found solace in the ever-shining light of the moon, which seemed to unconditionally provide her with love and care.

A week before the exam, Lily started reading a magazine daily to relieve her stress and pressure. There she read a story, a small chapter of a book called "Little Women," written by Louisa May Alcott. That was when she read the most important quote of her life.

"I'm not afraid of storms, for I'm learning how to sail my ship."

From then on, she started enjoying herself. Just before the entrance exams, she went to a party with her friends. She was asked many questions.

"Lily, isn't your exam tomorrow? Why are you here?" "Lily, don't you have to study for your exam?"

The girl waved away the questions, saying only one thing, "Oh, leave it! I'll face tests in life that are way more difficult than this! Nothing is going to stop me from acing this exam!"

The next day, Lily reached the hall with her head held high. Before the exam, she didn't even think about the questions that would probably come in the paper, and she paid no heed to the chattering students around her, talking about the chapters. When she received the paper, she almost laughed. She knew everything! But she took her time. When the exam was going on, she looked at every question and read it carefully. She finished the paper in three hours. Oh, what an exam it was! She skipped and jumped on her way home. She met with her friend Lucy and shared her excitement. Lily couldn't wait for the results.

One month after the exam, the results came out. Lily couldn't believe her eyes, and her parents were overjoyed. Lily had scored the highest in the state!

"We knew you could do it, Lily! Your hard work has finally paid off! We are so proud of you!" Lily's father said. Her mother was crying, and Lily hugged her parents, beaming at her success.

She looked at her desk and the open storybook. "I have sailed my ship," she whispered to herself.

As she closed the book and stood up, Lily thought about the challenges she had faced in life and how she had come out victorious in each case. How she had smiled in the face of despair and scored the highest in the whole state. She knew that she had accomplished what had been a dream for other people. She knew that she had sailed her ship.

The Terrors of the Mountain

by Rishap Sahoo

The beautiful orange sunset eased her peace of mind. After a long day of collecting vegetables in the mountains, Kanoe had come to her favourite place on the mountains. She gazed in the direction of the sinking, golden ball of fire and wondered what the mountainous terrain looked like without the warm light of the sun. Kanoe had asked her grandfather about this many times, but he had always avoided the question. Whenever she went down to the village, she would inquire about the nights in the mountains.

The kids ran away from her upon hearing her question. The adults would glare daggers at her and ask her not to speak on that topic. The elders' faces would contort into a fearful expression, replacing their serene and placid smiles. A few people told her that she, being so young, should not be exposed to the horrors of the night sky. "Demons," they told her. But even they were nervous, and the fright in their eyes was visible, as if the so- called 'demons' would appear out of thin air and gobble them up. She remained quizzical about this piece of knowledge. There was an underground asylum in the village. It was described as the quarters of the people who were deranged after luckily surviving a night outside the safety of their homes. Kanoe had once tried to enter to get some information about what happened after sundown. But she was prevented from entering by the gatekeeper.

"Kanoe!" A voice shook her from her thoughts.

"Come back quickly! The sun's goin' down!" yelled her grandfather. "Coming!" she exclaimed.

As they sat down for tea, Kanoe took out some slightly yellowed sheets of paper. Her grandfather watched her fold the sheet of paper while sipping his tea.

Very soon, in front of her, lay a beautifully folded paper bird. Her grandfather was always fascinated by her creation. Kanoe took a few big gulps of milk, contemplating whether or not she should jump out and throw open the curtains for her first look at the night sky. She decided she would.

Getting up, Kanoe walked over to the window, and with a triumphant 'ah hah', she threw open the window. It was boarded up from the inside with a thin plank of wood. Her grandfather stood up, his brows furrowed in worry and rage.

"Kanoe. What is the meaning of this?" he said, his deep voice beating her eardrums like tsuzumis.

"I... I just wanted t...t...to s-see the night sk... sky." she stammered.

"Kanoe, we talked 'bout this," her grandfather said it in a soothing tone.

Kanoe steeled her nerves and exclaimed, "But I really do want to see the outside world at night! Why do you always try to prevent me from just taking a look?" She rushed to her room and fell asleep instantly.

She woke up the next day to see that the house had been completely redecorated. It looked more like a dojo than a place to mingle. Then she saw her grandfather. He was wearing a keikogi and had shaved his messy beard. He looked like he was ready to start training uchi-deshi.

"Kanoe, take yer breakfast, put on yer keikogi, an' meet me 'ere in thirty minutes," he said.

Kanoe did as instructed. Sitting in their traditional Seiza posture, her grandfather started talking. "I believe ye are old enough to understand the horrors of the night sky, eh Kanoe?" he said.

She nodded in agreement. "Well, those village chaps were correct. There are demons outside at night. An' the ones who are outside are eaten by those monsters."

Kanoe looked at him in disbelief. Chuckling, her grandfather started, "Back in my day, I was a member of the Demon Slayer Corps. We used to slay demons left an' right. But once the stronger members took to retiring, the Corps was wiped out by those devils. Now, they just roam around freely. These mountains are infested with them. I shall train ye to fight them."

Kanoe was starting to get excited. She eyed the red, black, blue, green, and gold blades with a gleam in her eye.

"Let's get started!" her grandfather exclaimed.

Two years later, she was able to fight boldly with her katana. She had chosen one that looked pretty normal. But as soon as she picked it up, the Nichirin blade turned a shade of crimson and a dull blue. The blade looked beautiful. Like fire and water being held together. But in her mind, she was set on reaching her goal. She was going to kill the demon king that had terrorised the mountains all these years.

"Kanoe, come talk to me before ye leave, eh?" her grandfather said from behind her. Kanoe nodded.

As they sat down for some breakfast, her grandfather handed her a ghostly white stone.

"It's a Soul Jade," her grandfather said. "A human's power is nothing compared to a demon's. That's why us hunters use these stones to boost our power."

Kanoe seemed quizzical. "Are they magical?" she asked. "Well, as we used to say, a lil' bit o' magic can take ye' a long way."

The mountainous terrain was beautiful and serene, compared to the dust-clogged cavern inside the mountain. "Who dare to enter into my home!? Be my food!" a voice roared from in front of her.

Kanoe took notice that the demon could not see her. With sure and soundless steps, she crept towards the voice in an arc. The demon king was seated on a throne made of human bones. He had blood-red skin, two gigantic horns, and was surrounded by a scarlet aura.

Kanoe screamed at the top of her lungs and launched herself towards the demon's head. With one swift stroke and the magic of the Soul Jade helping her, she cleaved off the demon's head. As the demon disintegrated, Kanoe exited the cave with a triumphant smile.

Now, everyone experiences the night without fear and celebrates the defeat of the demon with theatrics.

Glossary:

1. Tsuzumi : A Japanese hand-drum

2. Keikogi : Traditional Japanese martial arts training uniform

3. Uchi-Deshi : Japanese term for Japanese martial arts students

4. Seiza: Traditional Japanese sitting posture where the person is sitting with him/her legs folded beneath

5. Katana: A Japanese curved sword

6. Nichirin: A fictional metal by which katanas are made to kill demons. It changes colour according to the wielder's strength, skill and personality. Red represents extreme skill and strength, whereas Blue represents purity.

7. Soul Jade: A fictional gemstone which is obtained when demons are killed

Your Hands Banish the Rain

by Aryana Perera

Tiny folds by the left ear, surprisingly an upturned nose, supple skin gripping onto a weak jaw. An unformed temple canvased by more skin. Soft all over, warm all around. I take your hands, you take my pinky, when we touch, we finally find each other. I don't have to search. I know that you're mine by your hands. I trace along each of your little fingers, I travel along the shallow auburn creases within the pulse of your palms. I try to savor every touch, I try to remember that wonderful milky newness in your smell, all the perfectly familiar distinction in your skin, how much I love when you cling on to me so tightly, even now, in a hushed desperation, in a longing fear. For even you know, what comes next. You know that I can't hold onto you any longer.

But I must cling onto you, for just a moment more. The warmth of dawn cracks the sky above, as the clouds profess their disgust: as the rain falls. It bites at me. I flinch. The droplets are hostile, boiling, they sear my neck as they drip down my shoulders. I remember the last time they felt this way. The rain begins to flood my senses, but it dares not drown my memory.

I remember how I reached out, trying to grasp, trying to hold onto anything in the shifting darkness. I remember the crowded voices, all the figures of shadow and light, reeling away from me, sudden footsteps silently retreating. Turning away as I face your mother. Your mother on the floor. With her wrists bleeding out, they tell me. I crouch down beside her; I kneel in the murky bathwater spilling onto the floor, the faint crimson streaks of blood within it, disperses to find me. They stain more than my clothes. I hear her breath, shallow and wavering. For the first time I pray that you're okay; I pray that you're putting up a fight. I then imagine your mother's eyes: possessed with self-loathing, consumed with a wrathful remorse. But searching, searching for her reason behind the cuts on her wrists. She stares at her womb and then she turns to me.

The rain batters down.

The water once again displaces me, I am a victim of its force. I writhe beneath its wallowing tide; I gasp for air as it forces me under. Under a past, I would much rather die than relive. Under memories that make what I'm about to do to you that much more sinister, that much more unforgivable. I struggle and fight, still the tide takes me under.

It washes me up unto that brutal monsoon morning, of the very same day this rain had begun to fall. The last day that I would see your mother with her wrists still intact. The same day I had pleaded with her to get rid of you. I remember her wailing, as I suggested the doctor.

I remember her cries, the sheer power of pure anguish in her voice, and how it had bounced off the walls, bounced off me. She could never come to terms with how her own womb had betrayed her. How it could conceive a child she knew she couldn't provide for or raise, with a cripple she no longer loved. A man that couldn't see her marring heartbreak in choosing to either abort or abandon the baby she once never wanted but has now nurtured for months in an intangible love. The baby she unfortunately shares with a man who couldn't see.

This life had trapped her. She could feel the walls closing in. Closing in some more, as I tread close to her. I follow the whimper in her voice. She retreats from the whiskey in my breath. I prod my finger in her chest and demand that my mistake be erased. The venom in my voice causes her to tremble. She shakes her head no, so I drive her out. Out of my house, out of our lives, out of your hands, out of her sanity. The next time I find her- I find her on the floor.

The storm ceases, its journey is complete. The guilt I had tried so desperately to drown is the only thing that surfaces. But the rain leads me back to you. Back to your wonderful little hands. Back to you in a wicker basket that I'm supposed to abandon come dawn. I trace my fingers along your back, I feel the curve in your spine. The curve that cripples you, the curve that says that I can't have you anymore. The curve that tells me the blindness will return.

The blindness that surrendered when you were born. For all my life I had been lost in the shadow, betrayed at birth by the darkness I would grow to fear. Until you came along. Until you made me see for the first time the love that I had been denied for so long, cuddled up in a warm blanket, tugging at my little finger, yearning to be loved just as I had all my life.

Oh, how can I bear to leave you? My heart bleeds. I'm sobbing now, I mark you with my pouring guilt. I hold onto you as tight as I possibly can, but the tide forces us apart. The rain compels my choice.

And I choose to return to the dawn still a father. I don't need eyes to know that I can't bear to live without you, this darkness can't blind me from seeing the future I deserve with you. The future in which we can hold onto each other for the rest of our days. The life these waters can never displace. The life I sanctify within our hands. The life that I promise you now. The heavens shine down us, as the flood within me finally subsides.

Your hands banish the rain.

Death of Louis

by Akshobh Atreya

"PROMISE ME YOU WILL REMEMBER, YOU ARE BRAVER THAN YOU BELIEVE, STRONGER THAN YOU SEEM, SMARTER THAN YOU THINK" – WINNIE THE POOH BY A. A. MILNE

It was a hot, humid day and the overworked slaves were scurrying around like restless mice carrying out orders of the unforgiving King Louis V. Everybody in Congo were well aware that King Louis was a ruthless leader, who only cared for a chosen few people. Meanwhile, in Brazzaville, there lived a poor, yet brave boy named N'kite. He was eleven and he was one of the youngest slaves of King Louis' slavery tribe, who were allotted to the construction of a colossal palace in the countryside. His loyal friend and fellow slave Makele worked right beside him. Both boys were exhausted with blistered feet and parched throats after having tirelessly carrying what could have easily been the hundredth trough of clay brought to the construction site.

"Why do we have to build a palace for the king's cat!" groaned Makele watching his friend grunt whilst lifting the heavy trough. Some of the other slaves helplessly stared at Makele for a fleeting moment and returned to their mundane task.

"Let's just do it, anyways, how hard can it be?" N'kite exclaimed rhetorically loud enough for everyone to hear.

"Lunch break! Everyone, here, now!" shouted one of the guards. They all ran frantically to the meet spot and gobbled down their tasteless, frugal meal, knowing very well that there will be no food until nightfall. They usually had beans with a scrapping of rice and bread but on special occasions they were given a small piece of meat.

"Hey, I'm tired of serving this king. Soon it will be Louis the VI then the VII and so on. I say, let us end this line of torture!" whispered N'kite.

"Shut up N'kite!" hissed Makele, fearing that one of the guards could overhear and they might be thrown into the dungeons.

"No! Enough is enough, we always talk about this, but we never do it, we might be slaves, but we are brave!" urged N'kite. Makele thought about it for a moment. His friend was correct, they had been bickering about these tough times for a while now.

"I'll admit, our previously discussed ideas are very strong, but if we're caught, we'll be sentenced to death!" N'kite went on, seeing the mixed reactions of fear and excitement in the eyes of all the other boys, especially his dear friend Makele, who now looked more determined than before.

"...but if we're not captured..." continued N'kite, sounding fiercer, "we don't have to serve him anymore, we will be ending this line of tyranny," said N'kite, thoughtfully, knowing very well that King Louis V had no successors yet! Makele and a few other boys now started getting interested in this escape plan, because they knew that a glimmer of hope existed in N'kite's confident words. They started feverishly chatting amongst themselves, then came to a sudden stop and unanimously agreed to the plan.

It was now decided.

On that chosen night, the treacherous king will be dead...

The sky had taken to its dark side. Nightfall came, engulfed in its own stillness. The surroundings were now deserted, and the air was calm and clear. N'kite gestured a signal asking the boys to run to the nearest gate. It was change of guard time. There weren't many guards around. This was a pivotal moment for them to make a rush, however, unluckily for them, two guards were standing in front of the main palace gate. They anticipated this and one of the instructed boys grinned sheepishly at the rest of the group and slowly brought a pan from his pelt bag. With all his strength and might, he flung it across the courtyard with perfect aim!

The guards were startled and immediately ran in the direction of the noise. Swiftly, the gang entered the castle gates and into the stillness of the open front yard. When they entered, there were two vast hallways.

"You boys take left, we'll take right," whispered Makele in a hushed tone. N'kite nodded in agreement, and they split up into two small groups and were ready to move ahead with their plan. N'kite and Makele remained together.

The passageway was convoluted and was cast in stone and hard cement. The open hall was pitch dark and the only thing they could see were each other and some faint light ahead.

They stealthily inched towards the light and were now faced with a section of wall and a mighty bookshelf.

"One of these books must open up the bookshelf to reveal a secret passage but which one?" N'kite asked himself, feeling anxiety rush down his spine. The duo scrutinized every book until Makele accidentally pushed a brick on the adjacent wall. It felt off place and loosely embedded! Makele tugged and pulled it until it budged. The bookshelf opened at its middle!!

It took a bit of time for the boys to discern the insides of the room they were in. When their eyes accustomed to the new darkness, a large, decorated bed popped up in their view and on it was King Louis sleeping soundly. N'kite took a knife from his pocket and did what he had to do! It all happened in a flash and when the end came to be, the boys felt a reassuring sense of relief, but were still in shock that they had carried forth what started off as a wild thought and had manifested into well-laid meticulous plan which had now given them the freedom they yearned for!! They ran back to the entrance and found the others, who had worked well in the background, keeping palace guards and other distractions at bay. The boys were arrested and sent to prison that very moment. They knew this end would come but they also felt relieved that King Louis was no more.

In the morning, the Chief Minister came to N'kite and handed him a scroll. N'kite was terrified that the worst had arrived, and he was issued a death sentence. With trembling hands and tears running down, he opened the scroll and he read...

Thank you for your act of bravery. You have done what none of us have been able to accomplish! You are now free to leave these palace grounds, not as a slave, but a free citizen. On one condition...
"Promise me you will remember to be as brave and as strong as you are now forever."
The Minister.

N'kite was exasperated, shocked, and stunned! The tears rolling down his cheeks were now of utmost joy. He screamed with joy. All the boys took turns to read the scroll and were all crying in joy now!

It was break of dawn now. The boys walked out of the palace gates into the city, a land which they had never seen before. Their limbs ached, their stomachs were roaring with hunger, bodies covered in scratches and hearts ebbing with happiness. Each one of them reflected upon their brave act and swore to each other that wherever their free lives took them, they will continue to be brave and strong for as long as they lived and walked this free earth!

The Fly Past

by Naysa Dsouza

On a beach in England, where shore crabs crawl through rocks and where rocks cover the sand, where the sand is damp from the high-tide sea and where the sea reaches out to touch the sky, on the shore of this beach I stand, soaking up the good weather.

Ocean surf flows to and fro toward the boulder where I was perched, lapping up the grainy sand and tickling my toes. A beige crab scuttles across a smooth, large pebble, skirting around the water, which is slowly devouring this portion of the beach.

Then, something changes. The atmosphere isn't calm as it used to be. A feeling of anticipation hangs in the air, but I don't feel scared. Somehow, I feel rather curious. What's going to happen? Rocks around me start trembling, quivering side by side. I stand up, hearing something. A droning sound, crescendoing.

All of a sudden, an airplane zips past, leaving a trail of smoke in its wake. A grayish-green one with the camo print, the type from the army. Temporarily blinded by the cloud of smog, I feel my way back to the boulder. I was just a meter away from an army plane! My hair dances crazily, happily, excitedly in the rush of wind that followed the plane. After years and years, I feel thrilled, overjoyed, and just like a child, like the breeze that made my hair dance has the power to make me dance too. So, for old times' sake, I throw my arms up into the fresh sea air, run into the ocean blue, and twirl like I have no care in the world, laughing my worries away.

But then, like the plane, that fleeting moment is gone and reality crashes back onto my shoulders.

I slump back to my rock, the enthusiasm and energy seeping out of me slowly but surely. Why couldn't that moment have lasted forever? Why do we have to grow up? But, no matter how upset I feel, I know that that moment was the silver lining to my day. That window into my past reminded me what it was, and is, to be a child, and why I should have treasured every day, every minute, every second of my childhood.

I cheer up, feeling brightened. Patches of seaweed grass still wave gently in the breeze left behind and the surface of a tide pool still ripples, and so, I decide that I too will still enjoy this feeling of being a child, as long as the ocean touches the shore.

Wonders of the World

by Usman Bokhari

'THERE IS A WHOLE LOT OF THINGS IN THIS WORLD OF OURS YOU HAVEN'T START WONDERING ABOUT YET.'

B- BANG BANG! Creaked the old crooked door behind us. It happened when we were sitting on the silky couch, hunched, watching television. It showed us scientists stirring and mixing potions randomly, which made zombie virus, and someone touched it.

BANG! BANG! BANG! Banged the old door repeatedly and furiously. We went to the glass hole in the middle of our door.

Ibrahim's tousled hair stood up, his eyes didn't move not even what looked like HALF a millimeter. His teeth chattered vigorously, he was dreadfully silent and his body trembled. Ibrahim was wearing an aqua colored shirt, his skin was soft melted butter, and he smelled like a red rose.

'NO!' Usman thought. "This is not real! 'ZOMBIES!'"

'Let me see!' Let me see!' yelled Aisha. She pushed Usman from the way.

'H-ey!' I stammered.

'Remember the wall to space?' asked Ibrahim, suddenly. 'Let's exit from there.'

'Ready the vehicles first,' I ordered firmly. "Quickly! This old door won't hold us for long.'

He hopped in the seat, and made the engines ready, and got the handy oxygen masks. 'Hop in!' said the three.

'Ok!' I struggled across the messy room.

'The door broke! Faster!' Ibrahim cried. Zombies started pouring in like syrup.

'Made it!' I heavily breathed like an angry dragon. 'Goooo!'

The wall opened, like opening a crumbled paper and we fled through, but we weren't in space we were in ANOTHER REALITY!

'What?' said Ibrahim?

'I thought this world was made to make us go to space!' Nobody answered.

'The sky was as vermillion-red as an unpolished-ruby. Looking at the faces of people our body froze like we're paralyzed, sweat dropped from our face our eyes were wide opened. The people's nails were as sharp as the sharpest peek of a Mountain. Their skin was as wrinkled as a blood-red dragon. Their eyes glowed red like a shimmering, red gleam. They wandered like nomadic zombies.

But then another thought came to my mind as I pondered hard, my mind prickled with HORRIFYING questions. How will we escape?

When will we escape? Where will we live? Where is the bathroom? Where is water? Will we survive?

It was ferociously hot, but we were alive. We landed in a villa's roof; fortunately, it was flat.

'Let's go down,' I insisted. We leaped down. THUD! THUD, THUD, THUD! (Our jumps made a sound as: THUD!) The person living slammed open the door. A whisper came to my ear,

I know you're here, Filled with fear!

Come out, Come out, you can't hide,

I know you're in the house's roof side.

If you come you will DIE, Like a laying fry!

Don't be shy,

I never LIE!

Say good bye!

We all didn't move for a moment. Dreadful silence.

'CHAPTER 2'

Wonders of the world, Yet to explore

We flew away seeing the oceans as lava, the grass was as dry as hay, and the Palm tree's bark was scarlet. Mostly in the village were houses.

There were few farms growing with LAVA INSTEAD OF WATER. Aisha's grey hair flew gently as we fled across. Aisha wore a velvety frock, she had tiny freckles, and ocean-blue shoes. Talha was bald, with gloomy grass-green eyes. He wore a hard shirt, a yellow trouser, and also some freckles. As for me, I had a pitch-black hair excellently styled brushed. I wore a green, silky shirt, with a blue and white patterned trouser.

By observing this astonishing view, thoughts came to my mind, to explore more worlds in the infinite Space. The stars, planets galaxies, milky-ways, and more, like lightning is eight times hotter than the sun. This also sparks an idea in my mind if I can go to the parallel universe and explores more to help me resolve the problems of the people of the earth facing.

Space is full of mystery

To find out more, let's study history.

The stars are glowing and sparkly dots, In the Universe there are lots.

Let's learn all the facts of the solar system, but can we learn more with wisdom?

The Universe is a vast space, I'm thinking the shape of space is a pencil case.

Black holes like to swallow up things, Maybe golden rings!

Black holes are very dangerous,

If you come close by you'll feel painfulness!

Start thinking about other things, No, not a person that sings!

This explains us, to start thinking about new thoughts.

We fled for hours tiredly, we saw a portal. Our hope rose and we rushed for it... we were in Earth!

Now the whole world depended on us, to finish up the zombies. WE HAVE A WHOLE LOT OF WORK!

A Revolution In Time

By Anam Mansuri

Leaving the footprints of her impact

She transforms the world

Revolutions she enacts

Screams of every voice must be heard

The velvet corsets, they say hide

The ignominy of femininity

How would the flooded chambers of

Knowledge see the light

It poses a threat to their masculinity

Such a formidable specimen is what we call women

Her mind possesses a strength

That could dust a thousand punches

Her voice possesses a whisper

That could silent every institution

The Hour of awakening

Shall be celebrated by dawn of a utopia

The orthodox of hating

Drowned in the caves of Macedonia

Breathing souls, arising from earth

Validating her disregarded birth

Unleash every side of her that is hidden

And you will find treasures in each of them labelled women

Battling against every judgement

Molding her body to suit their eyes

They make the raiment

They decide the size.

Yet, she bears the courage

To embrace her skin

The skin that became a shield against worldly damage

The skin that became a warrior when she was held hostage

The skin she wears is her ornament; every wrinkle paints an unseen image

Her conversations with the nocturnal moonlight

While the other half of the world dreams

Often include overlooked solutions to man's plight

She transforms the world into those dreamy scenes

Engraved in the bygone,

In the folktales we have heard

How a few thousands of them

Managed to change the world.

The Line Drawn on Sand

by Jovita Bhaumik

My life is like a line drawn on sand,
sometimes it feels like you are the wave.

You flow like water,
With grace and poise,
But you are dangerous
I can never predict your ploys.

You say you are see through,
but you are stained by the dark algae that lies
within you.

And the world?
They are your fishes,
Feeding off those lies,
so tell me,
Are you satisfied?

Your words were verisimilitude,

As if you were the victim that needed to be rescued.

Am I really the shark in your sea?

The villain in your story?

Your accismus to attention,

Is really starting to get to me.

You turned my entire world against me, That boat of trust?

It sank in your sea.

Because you drew me in,

In the middle of a thunderstorm Now I am under water,

And the line on the sand is gone.

My life was the line drawn on sand, Fragile,

But you didn't understand.

The line shimmered,

The line was admired,

Everyone wanted it,

The line was desired.

But the line was bleak,
When faced with calamity,
It couldn't withhold,
It was too weak.

Don't get me wrong,
It would speak,
But set to defend itself?
It was too meek.

You were the one,
That washed it away,
It was your sea,
Your wave.

But I'll take a hand,
I'll create the line again,
Your draconian cacophony,
Is destined not to stand.

The line is now made of gold,
It shines under the sun,
Glitters under the moon,
And it certainly won't crumble under hold.

Not that of a juggernaut,
Not that of your sea,
The line makes it all ricochet,
The line is a masterpiece.

My life is no longer the line drawn on sand, It is
now the pole that stands.

It tells the story of pain,
One of a heart
Once broken,
But never again.

The Color of my Mother's Love

by Nandini Aggarwal

These days I treat myself like a concept too, building up a beautiful character, built up like a religion, everything is meaningful and profound, and art.

I am a coloring page in black and white that the other people color however they would like.

The kitchen sink has been clogged for days, some utensil probably fell down there.

The honey milk coats my teeth, and the stars shine through the pollution.

my mother smiles, and i write a poem on the side. the color of my mother's love is meant to be the colors of the sunset's reflection.

she is the core of amber-coated sunrises.

I see her love on the sharp horizon, but wait- just..
just- soften the orange a bit on the right hand
corner- and that is my mothers love

i find homely comfort in the small joy of feeling
the shine of her sunset on my marble skin

my mother's love is dark gray- a hurricane that feels
like a hallucination, the color of the night sky.

she is the concept of divine darkness- a gentle night,
peaceful and comforting- a glimpse of pretty and a
greater beginning.

my mother's love, my mother's love
is the color light yellow-

the color of coconut oil-
she oils the cornerstone of our relationship,

and loves my hair the way the curious adore the
unexplored.

she oils my hair the same way nanu oiled hers, and
braids my hair the same way nani taught her.

my mother is an endless beauty,
a sky that changes faces-

i draw my mother with the colors she plants in my
life.

my mother is my favorite color

A Poetic Dissection Of Poetry

by Smritti Sridhar

it is particularly perplexing to try and convert

every action, breath,

movement, reaction,

glance, interaction,

conformation or romance

into a series of words just so they can be

criticized, patronised,

jeopardized, memorized,

glorified, testified and analyzed

but most importantly,

beautified and romanticized,

because we're poets,

we're sinners,

we think we deserve to smile at the world's sorrow,

preach about tomorrow in our skins

that are tattooed with today's vanity,

we light fires in our sane shelters and label it insanity

and leave the ones actually losing it to lie in the dust

they'll marvel at your words with laughter and tears

and soon they'll weather the same to rust.

poetry can be a lingering kiss,

a lustful whisper,

a liable irony

or a liberating truth.

but i'd say it's the most truthful at its youth.

because with time and tide,

our much vulnerable pride seeks the protection
of influence and its impenetrable hide

i still wish i could write as movingly as those

 soothingly beautiful teenage souls

what hooks my envy is that their lives look so
complete

and yet their descriptions of emptiness and
longing sound so scarily correct,

they command my deep buried desires to
resurrect.

one can never truly die with poetry in their
minds,

because you strive to create what you're told
you can never find

the concept of poetry is an elastic expression,
an easy kind of escapism

a viscous flow of heartfelt flattery

for the shadows of our much concealed realism.

there's poetry in the licking of my lips

the blinking of her lights

how deprecation drips from his appreciative
eyes

there's beauty in the grey of their white lies
the wonderful diversity of responses we give for
the same stimuli

there's a poetic dynamic in your still standing
guile

oh the courtesy of the curve in your straight
smile

i think greatly of myself as i pen these words

i'm higher than the clouds even if i'm a
flightless bird

there's a silent fluidity in my fluctuating ego,
but i let friction speak louder.

maybe i like my poetry kinetic and obstructive.

maybe i like my poetry sporadically destructive.

i let my words speak loudly at a safe distance
from my spectators.

may they strike a chord in those aching hearts

as i painstakingly pull myself apart from this
finesse of a farce

to become human again.

what if poetry is inhuman?

it doesn't matter as long as it is real,

oh all the things it can make one feel.

Just a Box for You

by Rachelmaria Padayatty

As the doors flew open,

I walked into the chaos,

holding close my box

Holding close my treasure.

A chaos that wrecked my dream,

The box,

a part of my dream. Weakening my hold,

The box separated from my hold.

I stood still, pale

As fear scarred my face,

shattered glasses,

bleeding palms.

My vision, at grayscale,

My expression, remain stale.

Chairs being thrown over,

Arguments displacing my thoughts,

A decade of me has passed,

And I am still standing here with my box.

Confused more than ever

panic filled the room,

pushing me

to the darkest of corners.

My box, no longer with me,

But hurled across the room.

Empty hands,

I have reached my doom.

What just happened?

Blurry eyes and forced sleep

I wake up to a melody

"Happy birthday to you, happy birthday to you."

Was I happy?

Was it all a just a nightmare?

Did i imagine it all?

Well, i see my box, far away, on the table

Happiness seeped through me and then it struck,

I opened my box

And my box no longer had my dream

But just a smashed cake.

Lucie's Adventures

by Sajini Varadharajan

- INTRODUCING LUCIE -

A girl who was happy,

A girl who was zappy,

A girl who was choosey,

Her name was Lucie.

She lived in Rome,

She loved to browse on Chrome,

She had so many things to play with,

Whenever she ate, she never wasted a single bit.

Her father, a kind man,

Litter and Pollution he used to ban,

A scientist named James,

Always famous for saving animals from forest flames.

Her mother, a helpful lady named Lily,

She was cool and forever lovely,

A patient nurse, who comforted every child,

Stayed by their bedside all the while.

Her house was very big,

Her balcony which had a growing wild fig,

It had five bright rooms,

You can never find a crack or a boom!

Her best friend- Leema,

She used to play with her and Seema,

Lucie always went to their house,

Leema also had a cute toy mouse!

There were lots of things to do in school,

Lucie swam in the swimming pool,

Her ambition was to become an ecologist,

With ecology, she clenched her fist.

- A PRECIOUS GIFT! -

Lucie's winter holidays had started,

Her dad built a new house, and Lucie departed,
She was fond of her toys,

And she loved playing with Rolls Royce.

Her watch bought by her dad,

It made her happy as it was a super add,

It came all the way from England,

She wore it for her stage concert during the
band.

Lucie loved it a lot,

How to make it glow, her dad taught,

She was walking and it shined in the dark,

Then she came across a tree bark.

Oh no! The watch slipped off her hand,

She needed it for one more concert band.

It rolled and fell inside the river,

Now no one knows who'll be the giver.

Lucie could not find the watch ever,

It was cold, she started to shiver.

Unhappily, she walked to Leema's house,

On the way she found the watch beside a jar
that had a small mouse!

- LOST AND FOUND! -

Lucie shouted, "Leema! Seema! Are you there?"

There came a sound like a bear,

It was Leema and Seema's band,

They picked up and gave Lucie's watch in her
hand.

Both were dressed up like bears and cats,

Wearing a suit with matching hats.

Lucie asked, "Can I accompany you to the band?"

Leema nodded, "Let's go to the bus stand."

Lucie kept the watch on the table,

She helped her friends by making labels,

They went to the bus stand and boarded the bus,

They made it to the concert without a fuss.

"Oh! Come on Leema and Seema!" Lucie yelled,

"B-e-c-a-u-s-e it's getting late," Lucie spelled.

After the concert they returned home,

Lucie asked, "Where's my watch? It was on the table alone"

"Let's look around," said Seema,

"Watch out there," said Leema.

As soon as they turned, the watch rolled away,

Time for an adventure, there's no other way!!!

- ROLL ON! -

The watch rolled off through the back door,

All of them followed it, they couldn't soar.

It landed again near the river,

Cold started making them quiver.

An old man picked it up and threw it on a
bridge,

This made Lucie think about the ice-cream in
the fridge.

A woman put it in a bed of grass,

Nobody knew when this running would pause.

It rolled away once more,

It stopped by a stick in front of a door, Lucie said, "I want to rest."

For over there, they found no pest.

They sat down tired after all the leap

All of a sudden, they heard a beep,

Oh! The watch rolled away,

Get up! Let's go! There's no other way.

Picking up the watch finally,

Lucie looked up happily,

Looking at a strange figure directly,

The three friends were taken aback suddenly!

- STRANGE! ISN'T IT? -

Lucie felt safe and said, "Hello!"

The figure wore a cape which was yellow,

Leema said, "Can you be our friend?"

The person didn't respond, but shook his head.

Seema whispered, "Is he saying yes?"

Lucie said, "Maybe he is, as his English is less."
The figure spoke, "I would be your friend," "Let's
all make a trend."

They were shocked that he spoke aloud,

However, he was looking sadly at the cloud,

They decided to hide him in Leema and Seema's
house, He was safe only in their townhouse!

It was blue, and they put him in a basket in the
jungle, Carrying him was a big struggle,

Finally, they reached home,

They covered the figure under a huge dome.

The figure returned Lucie's watch in her hand,
"Oh! Thank you for my watch band,"

They laid the figure in the bed,

They gave him an apple which was red.

- FRIENDSHIP IN THE AIR -

He did not eat any food,

Maybe he was in a terrible mood,

Lucie said, "I'll go home and get some water,"

Leema said, "We have to eat, don't forget the batter."

Lucie rushed home to see her mom up high,

She said, "Ouch" and looked at her thigh,

It was bleeding, Oh no!

When she got home, she looked out of the window.

Her mom noticed her thigh,

And asked her why,

Lucie told the story and when she fell,

Her mother treated her well.

Her mom told her, "These are aliens from a different place!

They look colourful; you can see their face,

They absorb sun's rays to get strength,

They are harmless and short in length."

So they became friends and named him Googly,
Googly showed them many tricks shrewdly,
They played a lot with him, happily,

He was a superstar, but missed his family.

- FUN AND RUN WITH GOOGLY -

The next day was Friday, a holiday,

They decided to do something and to play,

But they didn't have a ball,

They tried to search in the hall.

Leema searched and found a bat,

A teddy bear, a doll and a toy hat,

"Hmm! Let's play with this bat and hat,"

Leema said this pulling out a mat.

They found a toy badge, a toy spoon and a toy fruit,

They searched for the ball in the loot,

They played with the bat and the hat,

Seema found herself jumping high on the mat.

She looked at Googly, who raised his hands high in the air, It was magic, she was fair.

Googly showed magic, they were shocked,

The secret to Googly they unlocked.

They played and played all day,

Googly was fun, come what may.

It was great to play with Googly,

"You are good," they all said encouragingly.

- AN ENDANGERING DISCOVERY -

Lucie put on the TV to see the news,

They smelt perfume, does it diffuse?

What they saw shocked them,

The police found that an alien escaped from the
spaceship, we don't know when.

They had to send him back, they had no choice,

How? When? With which voice?

They thought that he was not safe on Earth,

He was safe on his planet where he had home
and hearth.

Hmmm.... Let's do something and see,

Let's create a program, which should be,

Lucie knew coding, so she knew what to do,

Lucie said, "I can make something new."

They ventured through Google about an alien,

Wait! They had to decide on a plan,

They discussed as Lucie went home,

She thought about aliens in Rome.

She went and told her mother about this,

"Oh mom, this is something I can't miss."

Her mom said, "Make a code…"

"A program? Yes, that I can afford."

- A PROGRAM TO THE RESCUE -

Lucie grabbed a pen and a paper too,

She had to design a code whether old or new,

Her mom asked, "Didn't you make it?"

"Where?" Lucie asked smiling a bit.

"In your computer of course," her mom said,

Lucie sighed, "Oh! That's lying in my bed."

She took out her computer and her watch,

She also took an instrument that looked like a torch.

She sat on her chair in her room,

Lucie opened the instrument which made a vroom,

She took out a very special wire,

And plugged it in like a car's tire.

She converted her program into her watch,

She put the wire back into the torch,

Now Lucie was ready to save the day,

She went to Leema and Seema's house to play.

Leema asked, "Where were you?"

She explained to her friend the code which was new,

Her friends agreed to send him back,

But the spaceship! Did they lack?

- ALL IS WELL AGAIN -

Lucie clicked a button on her watch,

Which Leema and Seema tried to trick the police swatch.

It said, "No detecting has been done,"

"What does this mean?" Lucie asked looking up to the sun.

Leema said, "This means that the spaceship has not yet come,

Oh! Seema lets prepare to run."

Now it showed a tick, means it has been found,

Lucie said, "Hurry! We have to be time bound."

Soon, the spaceship arrived there,

The smoke blinded all who came there,

"Thank you for all your help," the other aliens said,

"You're welcome," said Lucie bidding bye to Googly with eyes red.

They started to cry because they would miss Googly,

They ran again to him hastily,

They hugged him again and said, "Bye"

Googly went in the spaceship up high.

In their school, they received prizes,

Their humanity and kindness attracted lot of praises,

It became a normal life for all of them,

Their next mission might start,

we don't know when!!!

Envy

by Ananya Shah

I envy people who can cry whenever they want to,
Because all I can do is sit here
and hold everything in me.

I feel like the unbreakable glass,
searching for ways to break,
Why did you make me unbreakable
when all I want is to break?

I feel like I am asking for attention
when I look up at the rain,
drenching myself in it,
But all I am doing is wishing my eyes
were the clouds and the rain the salty teardrops.

I am silent and calm, composed and proper,

Because you do not see the storm inside me,

wanting to come out,

but afraid of the havoc it may cause.

They ask why I tell them, cry it out,

nothing will make you feel better,

How do I tell them that I only know this

because of how much the tears

are killing me from inside,

the salt slowly eating me away,

but they will never come out.

Oh how I envy people who can cry

whenever they want to,

because I can't and only I know how much it hurts.

The Foreseen

by Hanan Nazeer

It's Inevitable

Under the sky, pours down the night,

it seems cold and the air is light.

Drugs in wine.

The sweet smell of time.

It Feels euphoric and high.

The sky is dark and elegant,

the french motels are gloomy and fragrant.

The mirror is shattered and broken.

The soul of darkness is awoken.

The dark-eyed beauties looking pretty and fair,

slip the secret notes and letters into the mail.

But its too late,

through the room, I hear the steps faint.

The blood covers the sheets in the room.

The eyes are bloodshot with anger that fumes.

The moon is seen across,

it mourns the freshly new loss.

It's like all broken mirrors,

reflecting all the inner fears.

Suffocation

by Nitzana Susan Abin

Problems don't have an end

Solutions are part of our hope

A life where we pretend

Even when our journey is a downhill slope.

They don't let out their cries

Cause they made their heart assure

That the tears that leave their eyes

Will again be seen obscure.

All they want is an ear that will hear

Their pain and hardship

And will help them clear their bottled-up fear

And give them the warmth of a good friendship

The feeling is of a drowned body in a deep ocean

Gasping for a little bit of air

Through a trustworthy action

That won't hurt them even by a tear

Once these poor souls find them

They will tell them a story that was never told

And will cherish them like a priceless gem

And they will release all that they hold

They need more than kind glare

Or a sentimental heart

They want someone who will bear

Their pain and wont depart

Hand in Hand, Heart to Heart

by Sreepadmanabhan Vimalkumar

I saw him speed through the crowd

As he let go of my arm and ran across the street

He was lost amidst the throng, His cry reduced
my heart to pieces

He is my brother, my sibling and companion

I ran through the street, my eyes relentlessly
searching for him

Thoughts ran through my mind, clouding my
judgement

I stopped abruptly

He was very tiresome, the bane of my existence

His finger always pointed at me, though I was
never at fault

My mind hovered on the thought of leaving him behind

It passed away in a flash

Though irritating, I have come to admire him

His anguished wail pierced my heart

I remembered his heartbeat, close to mine

As we lay down at night

I relived his happiness and excitement

When I triumphed in school

I ran through the crowded lane, searching for him

I finally found him, his head resting on his knee

I consoled him, and walked back home, hand in hand

And it hit me that he is little.... a lot closer to my heart

Circus

by Andria Vinod

They laugh when they see me smile
Every time, I've been exiled.
It seems my life is a crime,
Is it so bad that I live a lie?

What is it that they like?
My face painted all white?
My sanity disguised,
Or my existence compromised?

Aren't I human? Aren't I a man?
Have I taken a path verboten?
Aren't I forsaken? Aren't I denied?
Unseen, unheard, a mere existence.

Step by step I walk on the tightrope

Unsure of what's to come my way

Their captious eyes watch my every move

I fight the urge to run.

They only see the clown

Not a grieving damned soul

Just the painted smile that covers

Heartaches and tears and pain and fears

Is that all they'll ever see?

Just the clown, the happy chap?

From dawn break to dusk

Like a hamster on his wheel

This endless lifeless cycle of mine

Seems to never come to an end

I guess that's all there is to me

What more do I need than the whole world in my
adoration?

What more than being

in the center of the spotlight?

Right, a normal simple gray life.

I suppose that's a lot to ask.

The Width of the Alleyway

By Emannuel Jose

Half past 11 in the night

young David is on his way home from work

Walking down the alleyway with a slight smirk

Thinking about his life and getting baffled by the stars at night

Trotting through the darkness

Unknowing of the dangers that lurk

Stashed in a ragbag his weeks' worth

All of the sudden ten eyes appeared

just above flat earth

bewildered by the eyes David ran back from the
way he came
An old man approached him and said

What is it son?

David had been gotten the fright of his life

The look of frustration and fear in his eyes

The old man understood

And he said do not be afraid my son

Those peepers are nothing more than

Some stray Whiskers wandering for food just like
you and I

So go David go home to your family in peace

And so he did taking the old man's advice

For he had been saved by the

Width Of The Alleyway

The Old Man of Hurray

by Shabil Mohammed Iqbal

There was an old man of Hurray,

Who worked as a carpenter by day,

When he was chopping wood,

The wood log stood,

And ran away from the old man of Hurray.

The old man, speechless, took off after the log,

On the way he met a crazed big dog,

'He took my bone!'

The dog said with a groan,

And thus on the streets were the man and the dog.

They chased for an hour on the roads of Hurray,

Till finally they reached a long highway,

They spotted the log,

Who jumped on a frog,

And swam down the deep blue bay.

The man and dog, refusing to give up,

Decided to call for some backup,

The man called his family,

The dog stood up valiantly,

And they swam down the deep blue bay.

Another hour passed, and without success,

The man and his comrades were in distress,

Till they reached a new town,

Which was named Countdown,

The man continued to sail in such finesse.

They finally tracked down the log,

Who jumped off and thanked the kind little frog,

And went down the lane,

Into a carpenter's domain,

And finally an axe chopped down the log.

The man and his comrades returned angry and crossed,

At the log that had filled them with so much exhaust,

They thought to themselves,

And took a log from their shelves,

Saying 'It is easier to chop ten logs than to chase down one that you've lost.'

The Dying Tree

by Tanuja Dulan Kumarasiri

Across the pond, I saw a beautiful tree.

It stood out from an endless sea

It called to me, grinning and smiling

We laughed and danced, its bark shining

The leaves sparkled with happy dew

The wind in our sails harder blew

I was so glad I didn't even notice;

Stuck in my love filled hypnosis.

The steel that bound me: awestruck

Me to the tree, now I was stuck

I sadly stood;

Bound eternally to this lifeless wood.

I struggled, twisted and turned:

Hope and dreams burned

My friends waltzed by

Some waved, some said hi

Then the rain came;

Soaking, drenching and cleansing my eyes

Removing the lie, and the disguise

The tree didn't care, it relished in the torrent

It never cared, nothing did warrant

Its bark echoed; hollow

My heart woe'd: sorrow

The steel tightened, its grasp unbreakable

The kindness frightened, pain unfadeable

Trapped in four walls, whilst greener trees

Sang with the chirping birds and bees

The birds had built happy nests

While the tree was infested with pests

Bound by steel; there was no hope

Bound by my soul: my escape was a rope

It met an end,

Though I had died long ago.

Surprise Yourself

by Gaurika Gautam

Are you ready for it?

Are you up to it?

Each day asks me this ..

Every day I take the challenge

Obstacles galore, endless courage

Power of smile and belief

Determination and hard work

Sound of my own breath

Circle of loved ones around me

So what am I afraid of..

Nothing. I whisper to my soul

Nothing.. I whisper to my soul..

Afraid of my own self my own self..

I have to fight my own fears

My own failures..

It confronts me..

So, What's stopping you ?

Not a loser not a quitter

Nothing beats me

Nothing defeats me

Push hard deep within

Their lies the victory

Get ahead of my own self

Surprise your own self..

Limitless will power..

my newfound friend

And where do I reach..

Can you see the change

the sweet scent of success

long dark lonely path

fear not fear not

screams my heart

my head with conflicting

thoughts what should I do..

surprise your own self..

surprise your own self

I look ahead and think of the time to come

How will tomorrow be

What does the future hold for me

I pray to God folded hands, ask for the best

I reply to my soul

It's the faith, trust and self-belief

The power of never giving up..

I look the other side..

Rays of sunshine glistening bright

Birds soaring high

Beautiful hues of the sky..

I see hope, lots of hope

Doubt's try to creep

Leave them behind..

A heavy breath

A long sigh

Will I make it...will I ace it

Its easier said than done

But surprise your own self

Surprise your own self

The tomorrow shines..

Is There No Place?

by Josh Mehta

Is there no Place?

Is there no place for a heart so pure in this society, so diverse,

This concerns me for this questions our very existence,

Does colour come before ethics,

Has humanity stooped this low, to regard a black heart over a black skin?

Is there no place for a tad of imperfection in this society, thought to be perfect,

This world experiences an urge to reason with the inherent standards of society,

Do standards not know their boundaries,

Or have humans just stretched them too far?

Is there no place for a plethora of aspects in this society of varied interests,

Why do people, all of whose creator is the almighty himself,

Have to build barriers and break bonds,

Can it not be so, that for once we look beyond

the barriers of society and at the person himself ?

Is there no place for the colour of diversity,

For the celebration of humanity,

How can mankind be so diverse in a variety of aspects,

Yet at a close inspect, possess the very same assets,

Is there no place for questions,

For hesitation, perplexity and incertitude,

Why do we, in this world, intrude, delude and conclude,

Why do questions remain unanswered, curiosities unirked, and pain unsaid,

Is there no place for a warm heart in this cold shouldered world,

For a listener, a supporter and a defender,

Why is it so, that the sole warmth many souls receive,

Is a product of global warming, while there is internal storming,

Is there no place in the ears of the masses, to accept this wake-up call, For this I say, there is,

One can be a part of the society, without the society being a part of them.

The Knight in Shining Armor

by T Hurairah Faatimah Muzammil

She fell, she broke, she crumpled,

They tried to pin her down, but she never crumbled.

While they mocked her and tried to pull her back,

She was steadfast in her track.

She was hammered at spots that hurt most,

Her ruin for them was a chance to toast.

When she ought to be fed by her mother,

She faced the stab by her brother.

As she awoke each day,

She saw eyes peering as if she were prey.

She stood tall to fight the stray,

For she knew nothing would be served on a tray.

In every dark dorm, she looked for light
The streak that shone before her sight.
She waited not for her savior,
To arrive in a shining armor.

She dusted down each time she fell,
Battled every hurdle without a yell.
She steeled her heart to face despair,
Fastened herself upon her mare.

The invincible spirit in her heart,
Of hope, bravery and her kind heart,
Will take her places no one will reach,
Where no one will stab and screech.

She will hope, she will fight,
Restrain with all her might.
She will rise, she will fall,
But, never fail her inner call.
She will be her knight in shining armor,
And, will never stop being the charmer.

How Can This Newborn Ant, Take Down This Mighty Tree?

by P. S. Rudrakumar

As I sat there in the lone, cold October fall,

I heard the rustling of leaves

When I took careful steps, gentle and small,

I saw a unicorn poised on the house's eaves.

The moment it saw me, it began to hurtle.

When it dashed, its sheeny blonde mane, waved with the wind.

And came to a standstill at a precipice slowly receding as an unhurried turtle.

I saw a gloomy black hue, where the void margined.

I closed my eyes and fell into the abyss.

The consciousness in me waned

As I touched the threshold of consciousness,

I saw a land of bliss.

It was heaved preordained.

There was a garden of million golden daffodils,

Covered in dew and surrounded by trees.

Standing upright on the parakeet green hills,

And dancing gleefully in the merry breeze.

From a frosty mountain, higher than the sky,

Emerges an untamed river breaking down any beaver's wall.

Then it flows to a cliff so high,

And falls down as a cascading waterfall.

I didn't travel across the cosmos; I just went back in time.

To travel to the era when the earth was free.

Life had, is and will continue to flourish every hour's chime.

So, how can this newborn ant, take down this mighty tree?

I'm Never Bored of English

by Divisha Khatwani

I'm never bored of English,

I'm always ready to learn.

My teacher explains it once,

I never have another concern.

Grammar is my favorite kind,

Punctuation, spelling, the others among.

Commas, periods, colons, quotation,

I have them at the tip of my tongue.

1 think it's weird that nouns have 4 types,

Or verbs always have something added there.

'Could' or 'Can', BOYS with a FAN,

Somehow, I never noticed or seemed to care.

On the other hand, literature's there too,

Shakespeare, his works and his famous plays.

The Taming of the Shrew is my personal fav,

With 'thy' used in every single phrase.

Literary devices used in everything,

Metaphors and similes used to compare.

Personification, onomatopoeia too,

Alliteration: Probably perfecting particular
pairs.

Reading is my hobby, my passion forever,

I'll always be ready to open a book.

Novels and dictionaries,

I'll read everyday pictures/drawings in books,

I'll look.

Debating, public speaking, talking.
They are a part of English too.
Rule of Three, Statistics, Speeches, Anecdotes.
Arguments from a different point of view.

My favorite part of English isn't grammar,
Or literature, or books I read, it's poetry.
How I express my emotion through rhymes,
A poem is forever my ideal cup of tea.

English, to me, isn't a language,
Nor is it a subject in school.
English is a part of my life, without it,
Sign language would be the new cool.

Just kidding, English will never leave my life, it rules, English never makes me bored, in all kinds of schools.

Thank you!

Printed in Great Britain
by Amazon

27791459R00126